alligator bayou

ALSO BY DONNA JO NAPOLI

For Young Adults
Beast
Bound
The Bravest Thing
Breath
Changing Tunes
Crazy Jack
Daughter of Venice
Fire in the Hills
For the Love of Venice
Gracie, the Pixie of the Puddle
The Great God Pan
Hush: An Irish Princess' Tale
Jimmy, the Pickpocket of the Palace
The King of Mulberry Street
The Magic Circle
Mogo, the Third Warthog
North
On Guard
The Prince of the Pond: Otherwise Known as De Fawg Pin
Shark Shock
Shelley Shock
Sirena
The Smile
Soccer Shock
Song of the Magdalene
Spinners (with Richard Tchen)
Stones in Water
Three Days
Trouble on the Tracks
Ugly
When the Water Closes Over My Head
Zel

For Younger Readers
The Hero of Barletta
Angelwings (a series of sixteen books)
The Wishing Club: A Story About Fractions
Sly the Sleuth Mysteries (with Robert Furrow)

donna jo napoli

alligator bayou

WENDY
LAMB
BOOKS

Published by Wendy Lamb Books
an imprint of Random House Children's Books
a division of Random House, Inc.
New York

Visit us on the Web! www.randomhouse.com/teens

Educators and librarians, for a variety of teaching tools, visit us at
www.randomhouse.com/teachers

Library of Congress Cataloging-in-Publication Data
Napoli, Donna Jo.
Alligator bayou/Donna Jo Napoli.—1st ed.
p. cm.
Summary: Fourteen-year-old Calogero Scalise and his Sicilian uncles and cousin live in
smalltown Louisiana in 1899, when Jim Crow laws rule and anti-immigration sentiment
is strong, so despite his attempts to be polite and to follow American customs, disaster
dogs his family at every turn.
ISBN 978-0-385-74654-0 (hc)—ISBN 978-0-385-90891-7 (lib. bdg.) [1. Prejudices—
Fiction. 2. Italian Americans—Fiction. 3. Uncles—Fiction. 4. Race relations—Fiction.
5. Country life—Louisiana—Fiction. 6. Louisiana—History—1865–1950—Fiction.]
I. Title.
PZ7.N15Am 2009
[Fic]—dc22
2008014504

The text of this book is set in 12-point Berthold Baskerville Book.

Book design by Angela Carlino

Printed in the United States of America

10 9 8 7 6 5 4 3 2 1

First Edition

For Maurice Eldridge

one

The night is so dark, I can barely see my hands. It's eerie. As if Cirone and I are made of nothing but air.

That's how I used to feel back in Sicily when I'd walk in the caves near Cefalù. I was nothing, till the bats sensed me and came flapping out in a leathery clutter—*thwhoosh*—then my arms would wake and wave all crazy as they passed by and away into the sea breeze.

But this flat meadow couldn't be more different from those hillside caves; this sleepy Louisiana town couldn't be more different from busy Cefalù; and I feel like a whole new person. I was a scaredy-cat boy when they pushed me onto the ship last autumn to come here. But now I work like a man. And I'm important at work, because I can speak English with the customers.

Still, some of the old me remains. Right now I'm jittery at being out late without permission from my uncles. It was my cousin Cirone's idea. It's always his idea. We all go to bed early every night except Saturday, but he's got energy to spare. He begs me to sneak out.

The grass is high here behind the lettuce field, but soft. It crushes underfoot, silent.

I follow close behind Cirone. He knows lots about this place. He's been in America longer than me. He came with his big brother, Rosario, when he was only four. He's thirteen; I'm fourteen; I edge in front of him now.

The slaughterhouse sits on the outskirts of town, at the edge of the woods. The place is lit up and we can smell the rot and hear the men inside singing as they work. Cirone heads that way.

"Shhh," Cirone says, even though we weren't talking. "They hear Sicilian and they'll chase us off."

I don't get why people here don't like Sicilian. Our family supplies this town, Tallulah, with the best fruits and vegetables. You'd think the sound of Sicilian would make their mouths water. Instead, we hold our tongues—or speak English if we can—in the presence of town people.

But not everyone minds hearing Sicilian.

That's how I met Patricia. I smile. She overheard Cirone and me as we unloaded crates, and she asked what we were speaking. She said Sicilian was pretty, like music. And she walked off singing. We've talked a half-dozen times since then. Always at the vegetable stand. I hear her voice in my head all the time. I'll be working, and there she is, in my mind, looking over my shoulder, saying something sweet.

I miss hearing Sicilian in the streets—jokes, arguments, announcements, everything that makes up life. Here the six of us are like mice on a raft in the middle of the sea. Oh, there are two more Sicilians in Milliken's Bend, five miles away—Beppe and his son, Salvatore. To find more, though, you have to travel down south to New Orleans, over 250 miles. Thousands live there.

I watch Cirone's shadow move farther ahead of me, out of whisper range. But here in the dark it's better to hush anyway.

In the woods now, we wind through pines. These trees are gigantic compared to the trees back home. They crowd out the sky so I can hardly see the stars.

In an instant Cirone is running, and I am, too. We dash for the open grass. No one's chasing us, but it feels like they are.

"Calo, stop!" Cirone grabs me by the arm and pulls me to a halt.

A giant cat comes out of the woods. Tawny brown

sleeks his back and white flecks his head and shoulders. He glances at us and pauses as his eyes catch the light: yellow-green. He flicks the tip of his long tail and I think I might wet myself. That cat weighs more than me.

The cat hisses low. Then he walks on toward the stench of the slaughterhouse.

Cirone's fingers dig into my arm. "A panther," he breathes. "They stay in the forests, away from people. It's special to see one so close to town."

"Special?" I'm shaking. In Sicily mountain wildcats don't even come up to your knees. "I can do without special. I can go the whole rest of my life without special."

"We did good. We did really good, Calo. You're never supposed to run from them. You just stare. A panther won't attack unless you look away. If you stare right at them, they think you're going to eat them."

I yank his arm, and we run. We don't slow down till we see our house.

Out front we hear a man arguing with Francesco in English. Shouting. The man stomps off into the night, throwing curses over his shoulder. Cirone and I crouch off to the side. It's so dark, all we can see is the tip of Francesco's cigar, glowing red when he sucks on it. And he's sucking fast. Red, red, red, red. He's mad, all right.

Cirone and I sneak to the back and climb in through a window. We quick move the sacks of pinecones in our bed that were doubling for us and stash them. We dive under the sheet fully clothed.

4

My heart still bangs against my rib cage. A panther. This place is full of surprises. Nasty ones.

I have to push Cirone's feet away from my chin. Mine reach past his nose. Feet stink, especially when you don't dip them in the wash pan before sleeping. But lying head to toe is the only way we both still fit in this bed.

I turn my head to the right and listen to the noisy breathing of Rosario, Cirone's brother, in the next bed. He's thirty-seven, old enough to be Cirone's father. Rosario has a big beak of a nose and long sideburns. Cirone's nose is small like mine.

Beyond Rosario there's Carlo, in his fifties. And in the next bed, Giuseppe, who's thirty-six. Carlo and Giuseppe are Francesco's brothers. Francesco, the youngest, is only thirty, but he's the leader. It's his nature. He sleeps in the bed closest to the door—the first to face trouble, if any comes.

These two sets of brothers are cousins to each other. And then there's me. We're all from Cefalù, in Sicily. The men call me nephew, and Cirone calls me cousin, even though my father was just good friends with them.

Back in Cefalù I have a younger brother, Rocco. The spitting image of me. The one person alive in the world I know for sure I'm related to. When Mamma died last summer, there we were, Rocco and me, with nobody but each other. Our father disappeared years ago. The Buzzi family next door took in Rocco, but they couldn't afford me; I eat too much. They put me on a ship to Louisiana. They said

5

Francesco would take me in. My father paid his passage to America years before—it was time for Francesco to repay the favor.

I miss Cefalù, with its stone and stucco buildings; I miss the glowing colors of the cathedral mosaics. I miss the sense of how small I become when I kneel in the pews. The music in the public squares. The sharp-and-sweet spongy *cassata* on holidays, lemony, creamy with ricotta. The purple artichoke flowers in fields that go on forever. The smell of the sea night and day, wherever you go. How close the sky is.

I miss Rocco.

And most of all I miss Mamma. My cheeks heat up. My father left so long ago, I hardly think about him anymore. Lots of fathers went to America and never showed up again. But Mamma, she's different. The fact that she's gone still feels unreal. I hardly believe I won't see her till I join her in Paradise.

So it's better that I'm in America. I have a chance to make something of myself. That's what Signora Buzzi said when she packed my things and walked me to the boat.

The door to the bedroom creaks, and I hear Francesco undress and lower himself onto the bed.

Inside my head I see the glowing tip of his cigar as that man went off into the darkness. Red, red, red, red.

two

The next morning I'm slow because I took so long to fall asleep. I sit at the table with my chin propped in my palms.

Francesco picks up the shotgun.

Town people call Francesco crazy because he's quick to shout. They snicker behind his back in the grocery. I've never seen him act crazy, though. But when I see that gun in his hand, I think of the argument last night and that man cursing.

The others have gone on ahead to work; only Carlo's here in the front room, straining goat milk for cheese. He doesn't see the gun.

I nudge Carlo and jerk my chin toward Francesco.

Carlo's eyes widen. He puts down the milk bucket. "You shoot at Willy Rogers and the whole town will come after us."

Shooting anyone would be terrible, but Willy Rogers? Tallulah has over four hundred people, but only a few run the show. And Willy Rogers' father is one of them.

Francesco jabs his finger at Carlo. "Not if he shoots at me first."

"Francesco! Remember five years ago?" Carlo wipes his hands on his apron. "They lynched seven Negroes right on Depot Street. A white man started it, but no one asked who shot first. Don't do anything stupid!"

Lynched? Francesco winced when Carlo said that. What's it mean? But Francesco's already talking again, louder and faster.

"No one tells us how to run our business. Not Willy Rogers, not anyone."

"He's a boy," says Carlo.

"You're so old, you think everyone's a boy. Willy's got to be twenty."

Carlo shrugs. "What he said didn't bother me."

"Of course not. You went inside and slept through most of it. Besides, he said it in English and all you speak is Sicilian. But if you had understood . . ."

"I didn't. That's my point. I didn't understand. Neither did Giuseppe or Rosario. So we weren't insulted. We went

to bed peaceful. Give it another day and you'll feel peaceful, too."

"I don't want to give it another day." Francesco's face
goes purple. "If I let Willy Rogers get away with insulting
us here, at our home, the next thing you know, he'll do it in
public. We'll lose customers."

Carlo turns to me. "What do people say about our
fruits and vegetables?"

"They're the b-b-best," I stammer.

"See? No one's going to shop elsewhere because of
what Willy Rogers says."

"Oh, yeah? He said we're criminals. Like all Sicilians—
that's what he said—all Sicilians are Mafia. It's the same rotten lies all over again."

I jerk back at the word *Mafia*. Back in Italy the Mafia
men used to offer boys money to knock over a fish cart or
break a window. Little jobs—warnings before the Mafia
men did something more drastic to ruin anybody who
didn't do things their way. Mamma said that's how boys
got corrupted into joining them—she told me to run when
they came near. We're nothing like Mafia. How could anyone say that about us?

Carlo stiffens. "We run a legitimate business. Everybody knows. Words don't change the facts."

"Words like that give them the excuse they want. He
said there's more Sicilians in Louisiana than in all the other
states put together, so many we're running honest men out

9

of business. He said we're an epidemic; we should be wiped out."

Carlo's shaking his head. "We haven't given anyone cause to complain."

"He says I gave him cause. Yesterday."

Carlo's eyes narrow. "What did you do?"

"He came into the store—first time ever. A Negro walked in and Willy stamped out. Then he comes here last night and says our store is dirty because we serve Negroes. He says all Negroes are filthy except for the servants of the whites. He wants them standing out by the back door. And waiting till all the whites are served first."

Willy Rogers must be crazy. Negroes aren't dirty. Besides, half our customers are Negroes. You can't make half your customers wait for the other half.

Carlo's cheek twitches. "Telling us how to run our business."

"That's what I said. You see? You see why I have to stand firm? They have the whole town to run their way— we have our store. We decide how we run it."

Carlo's shoulders slump. "Are you sure we're not breaking any law?"

"The Jim Crow laws say you can't serve food to whites and Negroes in the same room at the same time. They don't say anything about selling it. We're just a grocery."

"They could twist the law."

"You know what the Negroes would think of us if we

told them to stand out back? Never! We do business with everyone. Good business. It's bad business to treat any customer without respect." Francesco's holding that shotgun high as he talks. "That Willy Rogers isn't our boss. We stop his mouth right now. If he calls us criminals in front of people, he'll dishonor us. Even people like Dr. Hodge will think bad of us. Then I'll have to shoot for real."

Carlo steps toward Francesco, shaking his head. "A foolish boy could take a warning shot the wrong way. He could shoot back—and aim."

"Bah!" Francesco opens the door.

"I'm still your big brother!" Carlo stamps his foot so hard the floor jumps. "Don't you turn your back on me!"

Francesco faces him. "I'd rather have my head shot off than have to hang it in shame."

"Have you ever known a fool to hold his tongue? You can just bet everyone knows all about your fight last night." Carlo sighs loudly. "Walk into town with that gun and you won't make it halfway to the Rogers house."

"I'm not going there. I'm going to wait by the railroad tracks outside town, where he always passes. If he apologizes . . ."

"When have you seen a white man apologize to a Sicilian?"

"I'm just saying, if he does, then one thing happens. If he doesn't . . . It's his choice."

Carlo twists his kitchen towel so hard, I think it will rip.

"We're strong, Francesco. We're strong inside. Let this pass. We need you running the grocery store, not out by the tracks."

"Don't worry about the grocery. It's all taken care of." Francesco leaves. He doesn't slam the door; he closes it quietly. That feels more ominous.

Carlo grabs my arm. "Go find that tutor of yours, that boy Frank Raymond."

Frank Raymond is eighteen. He's no more a boy than Willy Rogers is. "What's Frank Raymond got to do with this?"

"Nothing. But he's the only white person who seems to like us."

"Dr. Hodge likes us. He treated Rosario's cut a few months back."

"Bah. We paid him. It was a job. You go to Frank Raymond."

A quick shiver runs up my neck. "Do I bring him here?"

"No, tell him to get word to Willy Rogers not to go near the train tracks today. Anything—anything but crossing the train tracks. Hurry."

I snatch my hat.

"Tell Frank Raymond not to let anyone know the message came from us." Carlo drops heavily onto a bench. "And don't say a word about any of this to your uncles. Especially not Giuseppe, that hothead."

"I'll be late to work at the stand. Rosario will ask where I've been."

"What's the point of you getting all that tutoring?" Carlo shakes his head in disgust. "A fourteen-year-old who can't come up with a good lie in an emergency is a sorry sight."

I touch my lips. "I've got a whole pack of lies."

"Thank the Lord." Carlo closes his eyes. He makes the sign of the cross and ends with prayer hands shaking toward the ceiling. When he opens his eyes again, they're wet and bright. "I'm counting on you. Understand?"

"I understand." I walk backward fast through the door and fall over Giada, the baby goat. We both go flying.

Francesco's still in sight, halfway across the field. I take off running.

I pass the Rogers house, the second biggest in town. Francesco has picked a fight with their son!

Frank Raymond lives above Blander's barbershop on Depot Street. As I dash past the open barbershop door, Blander calls to me, "Hey you, boy! Where y'all going so fast? Looking for Mr. Raymond?"

I stop and catch my breath. I'm in a hurry; still, it's important to show respect. Blander knows I speak English. Besides, he's always nice to me. "Yes, sir."

He leans against the door frame. "You don't show your face hereabouts except on Sundays. You're acting like someone done something to you. That the case?"

"No, sir."

"My mamma didn't raise no idiots. What's wrong, boy?"

"Nothing's wrong, sir."

One side of his mouth turns down. "State your business, then."

"I just need to talk to Frank Raymond, sir. Quick, sir."

"Quick, huh? Mr. Raymond's done disappeared."

My cheeks go slack.

Blander smiles and claps a hand on my shoulder. "Just pulling your leg, boy. He's in that there saloon across the road. Stay here and mind the shop while I fetch him. Right here. Not inside—just in the doorway. If people come, say you reckon I'll be back in a minute."

"Yes, sir. Thank you, sir."

Blander crosses the street into the saloon.

I can barely manage to stand still. I tuck in my thumbs, and wrap my fingers around them, and look up and down Depot Street.

On the far sidewalk a lady and her daughter are watching me. It's Mrs. Johnson. She brushes her hands off as though they're suddenly dirty and gives me an ugly look. Then she turns her head and hurries her daughter away.

The way she brushed her hands, she must have seen Blander's palm on my shoulder. Rich white people like her don't touch Sicilians or Negroes. I feel all strange and slimy. There's crazy ways here in America, rules that

14

Francesco calls just plain stupid. He says to ignore them. But it's hard to ignore a woman looking at me like that.

Blander's not rich, so maybe he can touch whoever he wants. Still, I wonder if he's just made a problem for himself. Maybe rich people won't want Blander shaving their faces for a while.

But forget that. What to do about Francesco and that gun?

I look into the barbershop, where Frank Raymond's landscape paintings hang on the back wall. Blander lets Frank Raymond live over the barbershop in exchange for paintings.

What's taking so long?

I look toward the saloon. An enormous alligator head hangs from iron prongs above the door. Usually I glance at it, then drop my eyes as I pass. Staying on the very edge of the sidewalk, closest to the street. But now I stare, like Cirone and I stared at the panther. The ferocious mouth gapes and I see his yellow teeth. The story is, this alligator was caught crossing the road with a whole dead boar in his mouth. I believe it.

Alligators and panthers. And men with guns. Sometimes I'm glad my little brother Rocco's not here with me.

What is taking them so long?

Frank Raymond comes out of the saloon with Blander. His blond hair is bright in the sun. "Good morning, Calogero." He smiles at me.

"Good morning." I look at Blander. "Thank you, sir."

"I reckon you're welcome." Blander waits, all nosy.

I'm just about to jump out of my skin. I look at Frank Raymond. "Can we go upstairs to your place, please?"

"I don't have much time, Calogero. I have to get back to work."

"In the saloon?"

"Painting a picture on the wall."

"Can I see it?"

"There're no customers yet, so I guess I could sneak you in just for a minute." Frank Raymond turns to Blander. "Thanks so much."

"Ain't nothing to speak of. See y'all later." Blander goes inside his shop.

As we walk away, I whisper, "Show me later. You have to hurry. Please, you have to get a message to Willy Rogers not to cross the railroad tracks today."

"What are you talking about?"

"He can't cross in his usual spot."

"What's his usual spot?"

"I don't know. He just can't cross. Not going to work. Not coming home."

"How come?"

"I can't tell."

"Then I won't help you." Frank Raymond crosses his arms at his chest.

"Francesco's waiting for him with a gun."

"Oh, Lord." He rubs his forehead. "I'll take care of it."

"Really? Just like that?"

"Count on it."

Count on it. Just like Carlo's counting on me now. "How?"

"I'll figure it out."

"Thanks. Thanks! And, hey, what does *lynch* mean?"

"Lynch?" Frank Raymond blinks and his voice goes raspy. "What are you talking about?"

"My uncle Carlo said it, but it doesn't sound Sicilian."

"Let's talk about it at Sunday's lesson."

"Thanks. And don't let Willy Rogers know I told you."

"Then get out of here fast, because I'm sure Blander isn't the only one who knows you're talking to me."

"What do you mean?

"Every window is an eye."

I don't even dare to nod. "Thanks, thanks," I whisper, and run.

three

The day is passing too slowly. But quietly, thank heavens. It's been nothing but a steady stream of customers. Rosario and I keep selling lettuce and peas and spinach out here at the stand on the edge of town.

For sure, Francesco and Willy Rogers are both still alive. Frank Raymond came through for us. Carlo was smart to think of asking him.

And Rosario wasn't annoyed at my being late to work. He's been telling jokes all day, like always.

I'm starting to feel normal again. Well, no—not normal.

Actually, I'm starting to feel jittery all over again. But good jittery this time.

Church school let out half an hour ago. The closing bell rang just minutes after the public-school bell sounded off from the other direction. But I'm almost sure Patricia's still in there. It's Wednesday; she stays after for piano lessons.

The piano is on the ground floor of a two-story house. A family lives on the upper floor. The ground floor is the Baptist church. And the basement is the school. Unless it rains hard. Then the basement floods and school is held in the church.

It makes sense Patricia plays piano. She's always singing something under her breath. Her shoulders sway, her lips move. I saw the music in her before I ever knew anything else about her, except that she liked the sound of Sicilian.

She'll pass by on the way home if I'm lucky. I'm squinting through the afternoon sun up Stage Road, watching the church door. The windows are open, but it's too far to hear that piano.

"Calo, come," Rosario calls in English. In front of customers we're supposed to smile and repeat English after them and not worry about anything except counting cents.

If we're paid in cents, that is. Mostly, at Rosario's stand we barter. It's at Francesco's grocery store, in the center of town, that I have to be careful of the money. At least, when the ladies and gentlemen shop. They're the ones who use coins.

I used to work at Francesco's store every day, but lately he's wanted Cirone there so that Cirone can learn to handle money. I don't care. Out here I get to watch for Patricia.

"Calo! You hurry."

Two more English words. Rosario's near his limit. He understands what the customers say. It's speaking he won't do. Town people make fun of broken English.

Nothing bothers me, though. I practice English all I can. I started back in Cefalù with Gian Pietro. He had spent a decade in America. When my father left, Mamma asked him to teach me so that I'd be ready when Papà sent for me. Only Papà never did. Anyway, I could already say lots by the time I got here. And Frank Raymond taught me more. So while Rosario's in charge, it's me who deals directly with the customers.

"Afternoon," I call, rushing to help.

A white lady comes up to the stand with a Negro woman walking two steps behind. Why on earth is a lady shopping out here? The servant wears a kerchief covering her hair and tied under her chin, like the women who work in the cotton fields. The lady wears a fine dress and a wide, white shade hat with a rolled brim. She lifts her chin. Oh no: it's Willy Rogers' mother.

I glance at Rosario. He's not nervous. But he didn't see the gun this morning.

I feel like I've swallowed sand.

"Good afternoon." Mrs. Rogers smiles. I can't tell if it's real. Tallulah ladies smile even when they're ordering you to get off their property. But, at least, it's clear nothing bad has happened between Willy Rogers and Francesco. Yet.

I take off my hat. "What can I get for you, ma'am?"

"Them beans—the ones over there." She points.

Rosario throws a giant handful on a sheet of newsprint. He lifts his eyebrows at Mrs. Rogers, asking if it's enough.

She doesn't look at him.

"Is that enough, ma'am?" I ask.

"Double that. And okra. The smallest ones."

Rosario is already filling the order.

Mrs. Rogers watches with sharp eyes as the okra pods pile up.

"Good choice." I nod. "Tender. And the first zucchini of the season are in."

"Zucchini?" Mrs. Rogers wrinkles her nose at the word. I hold one up. "Green squash," she says. "Newfangled things." I don't know what that means, but I can see her eyes change. "Oh, all right. Give me some of them, too."

"And lettuce?"

"Rabbit food." Mrs. Rogers laughs. "Them bananas there." She looks at the fruit table. "How is it y'all got pineapples and grapes?"

"They come from South America, ma'am. Right through the port of New Orleans." I reach and pull out a spiky leaf from the top of a pineapple. "This one's perfectly ripe. Would you like it, ma'am?"

"Perfectly ripe," she mimics me. "How come you talk so fancy?"

"I take lessons, ma'am."

"From that white Northern teacher in the colored school? The uppity one?"

"No, ma'am."

She pulls back in shock. "Y'all ain't in the white school, surely?"

"I don't go to school, ma'am."

"Well." She fiddles with the gathers on her bodice. "Whoever teaches you sure don't sound like the good folk around here."

"No, ma'am."

She narrows her eyes, as if she suspects I'm poking fun at her. But I keep an open face. "So, ripe pineapples. But they ain't bruised up. And they came all the way from South America. How do y'all get them in such good shape?"

"We know who to order from, ma'am." I hold up a pineapple.

"I bet you do." Her voice is harsh again. She glares. "Them bananas is all I need."

Rosario tucks the newsprint packages of vegetables and bananas into the servant's basket. She smiles small at him, and then at me. I've never heard her name.

Mrs. Rogers drops coins into Rosario's hand, careful not to touch him. At least a penny short. Rosario puts a finger on each coin in turn, then looks pointedly at her.

She adds another penny. And, finally, another.

I work to hold in a smile; Rosario doesn't need words to run this stand.

The women turn to go.

"Thank you, Mrs. Rogers," I call. "Good day, ma'am."

Mrs. Rogers looks over her shoulder and blinks. "Y'all know me?"

Everybody knows Mrs. Rogers. And she knows that, of course. I bob my head. "Your husband is an important gentleman."

The corners of her mouth twitch. "Ah, you're the boy used to work in that other grocery." She half whispers the word *other,* as though she's talking about something bad. "You did good to change bosses." Mrs. Rogers nods. "You got sense. Next time I'll send Lila alone. You take good care of her now, grocer boy, you hear me?"

"Yes, ma'am."

Off she goes, Lila following.

I slap my hat back on my head.

"Yes, ma'am," comes a taunting whisper from behind.

I turn. And she's there, hair drawn into two braids that glisten in the sun. I grin.

"You ain't got to kiss her feet, you know." Patricia takes off her shoes and slips them into her cloth bag. She walks past me on wide brown feet rimmed with pink. "She got nowhere else to buy such nice vegetables and fruits now that her son Willy had that fight with your crazy uncle."

So that's why Mrs. Rogers came here rather than the "other" grocery—Francesco's store. And everyone's heard about the fight, and probably knows I visited Frank Raymond this morning, too. Everyone in Tallulah knows everything that happens in Tallulah.

As she leaves, Patricia looks over her shoulder at me in a way that makes my skin wake up.

"I'll be back." I run to catch up with Patricia.

"Hey!" Rosario calls.

I keep going.

four

"Mrs. Rogers is wrong," I say to Patricia. "Business is business. Francesco would sell to her no matter what her son did."

Patricia walks fast. "That ain't what she think. She just proud. She won't let her money go into his hands."

"It does anyway. We all share."

"All you Eye-talians." Patricia drags the word out.

I don't know what to make of that, so I ignore it.

"She believe what she want to believe, and I reckon a *yes-ma'am*ing boy like you ain't never going to set her straight."

"Are you mad at me?"

"Couldn't care less." She sticks her nose in the air.

I don't understand this girl. "Can I walk you home?"

"It's a free country. Besides, it look like you already is."

And all at once I don't know what else to say. We walk quickly. Patricia's bare feet make almost no noise, but my shoes crunch. Too loud. I wish she'd sing that song she taught me last time we met. But I can't ask.

We walk south along the edge of Brushy Bayou, out of town.

A startled bird flies up from the brush.

"If I only had a slingshot on me." Patricia blows through closed lips, making a blubbery sound. "That was a wild turkey."

I shrug. I don't like hunting. I don't have good aim.

"I know everything about birds." Patricia turns her head sharply, tossing a braid. "They's lots more turkey if you go north. You ever been north?"

I shake my head. "I only been south. I landed in New Orleans and spent a week there."

"A week in New Orleans," she breathes, impressed.

Guilt prickles my cheeks. "Well, actually, the steamship docked on Tuesday, the twenty-fifth of October 1898 . . ." I love that date. It's like a birth date in a way, the birth of my American life. ". . . but with all the inspections and questions, they wouldn't let anyone but first class off board until Friday. So, really, I was only in the city a few days, before . . . what do you call it? . . . sneak . . . sneaking onto a freight train to come north. It rained the whole time." I search for the right words. "Mud. All that mud slopped up everywhere."

She looks at me sideways. "You done talking yet?"

My cheeks flame. "I'm done."

"You sure? 'Cause that was some speech. Like a flock of geese, all landing at once." She laughs. "Your ship have a name?"

"The *Liguria*."

"Hmm. I'd give a lot to spend a few days in New Orleans."

"You will someday. You're getting an education. You'll do whatever you want."

"Where you from, sugar, that you think a colored girl can do whatever she want, with or without a education? That Sicily, it's some other kind of world?" Despite her words I see a smile in her eyes.

"Don't they teach you hope in school?" I ask. "A church school, and no hope? Baptists got it all wrong."

"That ain't no church school." She skips a few steps. "Colored boys ain't allowed in the boys' class at the town schoolhouse, and colored girls ain't allowed in the girls' class. So we use the church basement. Boys and girls together. A fine public school." She throws her shoulders back. "Course, we read Bible verses. At the opening and closing of the day. Like every public school."

I thought it was a Baptist school. Sheriff Lucas told Francesco that Italians aren't white according to the laws of Louisiana, so I wasn't allowed in the town schoolhouse on South Chestnut Street, either. The sheriff said I could go to the church school—Patricia's school. He advised against it, though. He said I'd be better off with no education. Or I could take a tutor, and he told us about Frank Raymond.

Well, Francesco couldn't have given a dried fig for Sheriff Lucas' opinions. And he didn't think I needed more schooling, anyhow. Cirone didn't have any. But, no matter what, he wasn't about to send me to a Protestant classroom.

That sounded right to me—I would never set foot in a Baptist church, for the sake of my dead mamma's spirit, which is as Catholic as spirits get. I had to keep up my education, though. Mamma would have wanted me to. She didn't let me quit school even after my father disappeared, when we needed money so bad. I had to keep studying. It was paying respect.

And now it turns out that school isn't a church school at all. Here I've been trading food and chores for lessons in English from Frank Raymond when I could have been spending the days with Patricia.

But Frank Raymond's done well by me. Besides, he's a painter, and artists know more about the world than most people.

Still, a real school is something else. With a real teacher. And Patricia.

"I think I'll come to school with you tomorrow. To sign up."

"Go ahead. Be dumb." Patricia lifts her nose.

"What do you mean? Then I could study with you."

"We get out for the summer at the end of the day on Saturday. Besides, I'm graduating lower school. And I don't guess I'll be going to upper school come September. I'll get my working papers. I'm the right age now. If I can save enough money from cleaning the church to pay for piano lessons, I can sure save enough to pay for working papers."

"What you doing, Tricia?" A boy a head taller than Patricia approaches. Two boys follow; they block our path. "You late."

"Like every Wednesday. Besides, it ain't your business, no how."

"You oughtn't to walk alone. Four miles. That's too long for a girl alone."

Patricia smirks. "Y'all see just fine I ain't alone."

"Right, honey," the boy says in a patronizing tone. "That's why you ought to walk with a friend."

Patricia shakes her head in disgust. "Calogero, meet my brother, Charles. He ain't always rude. Charles, meet my friend Calogero."

I hold out my hand to shake.

Charles looks at it in surprise. Then he shakes.

I shake hands with all three boys.

And no one's speaking.

29

"You best hurry, Tricia," says Charles at last. "Reckon we'll walk your friend back where he came from."

Patricia frowns. "You be friendly, Charles. All of you boys, y'all be friendly." She glances at me, then runs past the boys.

They step forward so that they're standing one on either side of me and one directly in front. I'm surrounded. Two of them are taller than me.

Charles looks me up and down. "You shake hands a lot, like some big man."

I wasn't trying to be a big man. I keep my mouth shut.

"Yeah, bet you don't weigh more than a hundred pounds with your britches off and your feet washed," says another one of the boys, "yet you proud as a dog with two tails."

They all laugh.

"That shaking hands—that's a dago thing," that boy says. "I seen it before."

Charles puts a fist on a hip. "That's a dago thing?"

I shrug.

"You like my sister?"

"Yes."

"What you like about her?"

I feel a trap, but I don't know how to get around it. "Everything."

The boy who's been silent all along steps forward and digs a toe into the dirt. "Tricia pretty as a speckled pup. I like everything about her, too."

Am I supposed to fight? I cross my arms at the chest like Frank Raymond always does. I know how to fight. But three against one . . .

"That's Rock," says Charles, jerking his chin toward the boy.

I nod at Rock.

"Strange name, huh?" says Charles. "He got it 'cause he stubborn. His mother call his head a rock."

"I have a brother back in Sicily named Rocco."

"Yeah?" This time it's Rock who speaks up.

"He's stubborn, too. And smart." I don't tell him Rocco is only four.

Rock gives a half smile.

I drop my arms and smile back.

"A little agreement over a name and 'stead of fighting, y'all suddenly conversating." Charles makes a face. "You dumb as a sack full of hammers, Rock."

Rock shrugs and looks at me. "I seen you working at the grocery."

"My uncle owns it."

"You must have too much work now and then, huh?"

I've never seen us too busy, but I nod. Cirone told me business gets wild by midsummer, when the fields are producing nonstop.

"Maybe you could throw a job our way. Just now and then, I mean."

"I could ask."

Charles shakes his head. "This is something, all right.

31

We in business together now." He laughs. "Well, how about this? Tricia going home to cook. You know what she put in the pot for supper?" His voice is a challenge.

I stare at him.

"'Gator." Charles smiles. "Still like everything about her, Mr. Calo-whatever?"

I nod, keeping my eyes steady. The image of the alligator head above the door to the saloon comes into my mind. Ugly as a pox.

"You ever eat 'gator?"

I shake my head.

"I didn't think so. I hear say you dagoes too dumb to eat 'gator." Charles laughs and looks at the others. "We got to remedy that, don't you think?"

"Sure do." Rock nods. "And the best eating, well . . . that's after catching. Right, Ben?" He looks at the third boy, who gives a nod. Rock puts his finger in the middle of my chest. "When the time right, we going hunting. 'Gator hunting."

five

I'm sitting at the kitchen table waiting. Somehow, all the worry of this day has left me starving.

Francesco finally shows up.

I'd hug him, but he's still got that shotgun in his hands. I keep my eyes on it.

"At last." Carlo makes the sign of the cross. "Thank you, Sant' Antonio."

Sant' Antonio is the saint you call upon to help you find lost things. I never prayed to him for a missing person, though.

Francesco rests the gun upright in the corner.

"Well?" says Carlo.

"Willy Rogers took a different way home." Francesco unbuttons the top of his shirt and makes a show of scratching his chest, but I know he's touching the crucifix that hangs around his neck. There's a small dove in the center— the spirit of the Holy Ghost. "He must have heard I was waiting for him by the tracks."

Does Francesco know my part in this? I watch their faces, but they don't look at me.

"Finished, then," says Carlo.

"He learned his lesson." Francesco drops onto a bench.

Carlo turns and dumps the pasta into the boiling water, as though this is just an ordinary day.

So that's the end of it. Squabbles in America end as fast as in Sicily. I've seen grown men roll in the dirt fighting, then lean on each other drinking whisky the next day.

"Go call everyone," Carlo says to me.

In the bedroom the others are playing cards. I poke my head through the doorway. "Carlo says to come."

We troop into the front room.

Carlo fills the wash pan with hot water from the iron teakettle. We dip in wash cloths and clean our faces and necks and hands, then sit at the table.

Rosario twists the tips of his mustache. All my uncles have mustaches that trail out to each side of their mouths. But Rosario curls his upward, while the others just let them hang. Cirone and I don't have mustaches yet, but Cirone's growing sideburns, like Rosario. Rosario points at the gun in the corner. "Someone going hunting?"

"Nah," says Carlo, serving the food. "Too tired." He gives me a quick look, but he doesn't have to. I know how to keep quiet.

Everyone digs in. We eat long, flat pasta—*pappardelle.* The same as most nights. They're the easiest shapes to cut.

Carlo does all the cooking. In a way he's the one who really makes us a family, 'cause that's what we become when we sit down at this table to eat.

The pasta is covered with fresh spinach and Italian olive oil that we order through New Orleans. So good. We finish and wipe the bottom of our bowls with bread. Then there's baby artichokes, fried whole. I eat and eat. Someday I should learn to cook. If I ever get a wife, maybe it'll help to know a little something.

Especially if she cooks 'gators.

I gnaw on the crusty end of the bread.

Carlo serves the meat. We have this kind a lot. Boys trade it for fruits and vegetables. Suddenly I sit up tall as the idea comes: "Is this 'gator?"

"Possum," says Francesco.

"What's that?"

"We don't have them in Sicily," says Carlo. "Long tails. They hang from trees."

"Nasty things that run around at night," mutters Giuseppe.

"But nasty tastes good," says Carlo. "Eat."

We don't talk much. After a long day of work, eating is too important to interrupt with words. We save talk for between courses.

We're just getting to the salad and the plate of batter-fried zucchini flowers when there's a thump on the ground out front. Then another. Then lots.

Someone knocks.

My eyes go to the gun in the corner.

But Francesco stays seated; he jerks his chin at me. I get up and force myself to open the door as if it's nothing special.

Joe Evans stands there, hat in hands. Three goats run around him, butting each other and chasing our rooster off into the bushes.

"Let him in," says Francesco in Sicilian. We don't have to use English in front of Joe. He works for Francesco in the fields. Lots of men work for Francesco on and off, but Joe's worked for him steady for a long time.

Joe comes in.

So do two of the goats—Bedda and Bruttu. Bedda's our oldest doe and Bruttu's our only adult billy. I herd them back out with my knees.

"No, no." Francesco beckons. "Bedda can come in. Not Bruttu. Just Bedda."

Bedda clambers over my knee and scampers to Francesco. He swears that doe understands Sicilian, and I believe it. I hold back Bruttu and shut the door in his face.

"Evening, sir," says Joe.

"Evening," says Francesco, switching to English. He rubs Bedda with a closed fist on the top of her knobby head, right between the ears. She lifts her chin to push up against his hand in pleasure. Francesco laughs at her and gestures to Joe with his other hand. "You want sit? Carlo get plate. Sit. Please. Sit."

I'm not sure Carlo knows the English words, but he understands. He gets up.

Joe stares at the bright orange zucchini flowers. "No, no, sir. Thank you, sir. Generous, sir. Much obliged, but no. I'm here on a errand."

"Wine? Whisky?"

"No, thank you, sir. I brought a message."

"I listen." Francesco folds his hands on top of Bedda's head.

"Dr. Hodge said enough. Your goats were on his porch again. He told me to bring them here. Right to the front door of your residence. That's what he said."

Francesco lifts an upturned hand. "That all?"

Joe shakes his head. "He told me you can listen to them tramping back and forth, back and forth." He rubs his chin, then pulls on his fingers. "He say it again: back and forth, back and forth. And he say it worse at his residence, because of his fine wood porch and all. They clatter on the wood. He can't sleep. Not a wink."

"He say his 'fine wood porch'?"

"Yes, sir. Exactly."

"The big doctor, he want go to bed now?" Francesco's mouth twists. "Now? Now is for eat."

"He ate hours ago." Joe's voice has a certain ring. I know he means that everyone did. That's how it is in America. And even we would have eaten by now if Francesco hadn't come home so late.

"Goat go where goat go. Is nature. Is how God want. Who can prevent?" Francesco shrugs. "Not me."

"Dr. Hodge say you got to."

Francesco leans back from Bedda and folds his hands in front of his chest.

"That's the message, sir." Joe's eyes shift nervously.

"No worry, Joe. You bring message. You done. I talk to doctor." Francesco turns. "Carlo . . ."

Carlo's already standing beside Francesco with a pile of okra. He wraps it in newsprint and hands it to Joe.

"Much obliged, sirs."

Francesco gives a nod.

Joe holds the bundle to his chest and hesitates. "And they's a second message. The doctor say he wants to talk to you tomorrow morning. At his office."

"About goat?"

"No, sir. About the gentleman Willy Rogers."

"Like sheriff." Francesco shakes his head. "Summons."

"I reckon so."

"You know what, Joe?"

"What, sir?"

"Willy Rogers, he want see you and me we no get nothing for our work, no money, no matter how hard we work. He want see us poor, like dirt, and never change. Everybody like you, you father, you grandfather, they slave before the war. Everybody like me, from other country. He want us go to him for help. Like children."

"You talking about them new voting laws," says Joe.

"Right. Right, Joe."

I listen carefully. Francesco often invites hired hands to come around on a Saturday night, but only once since I've been here have any come—a few weeks back. Francesco sat drinking wine, with them drinking whisky, and everyone smoking cigars and complaining about the new voting laws. I didn't pay attention. I should have, though; I sense that now. I move closer.

But Francesco just wags his finger at Joe. "So now you know. Willy Rogers, he no gentleman."

"I reckon he ain't, no, sir."

"And he not want us be friend, because friend, they help. You know? I help you. You help me. We should be friend. Who care what Willy Rogers want?"

"Yes, sir." Joe looks across the table at all of us. "Much obliged."

"And, Joe." Francesco leans forward and his face softens. "You know what friend do? Eat together. Dance together. Have fun. You understand what I say?"

"I reckon I do, sir."

"Down in New Orleans, we all dance together. Years ago. Why not here? Next time I invite, you come? Maybe you come next time?"

"If I ain't too tired from working, sir. Y'all have a good evening now." Joe backs out the door.

Francesco puts his forehead to Bedda's. He kisses her on the nose.

"Come sit down," Rosario says to me and Carlo, switching us back to Sicilian.

"Right," says Carlo. "The food calls."

It's a relief to use Sicilian; everyone can talk. I wonder how much each of them understood.

Rosario heaps salad on his plate. "Did you see how surprised Joe looked at seeing our wild greens? And the zucchini flowers. People around here have no idea how good they taste."

Francesco points at Cirone and me. "Pay attention, boys. Eat whatever grows. Save and don't waste. That's how to get ahead."

I take a huge helping of salad. So does Cirone.

"That Joe . . . ," says Rosario. "He sees what the new voting laws are about. He knows they're trying to keep us all down."

"The voting laws!" Carlo looks at Francesco in alarm. "What are you thinking? You trying to organize the Negroes?"

"A little honest talk, is all," says Francesco.

"A little honest talk?" Carlo's got his hands on top of his head, on his bald spot. "The whites will say we're causing trouble. Next thing you know, they'll say we're going to organize strikes on the plantations. They'll be afraid we'll burn down cotton gins, like those Sicilians burned the sugarhouse in Lafourche Parish. Then they'll really have a reason to run us out of business."

I drop my fork, I'm so flustered. I open my mouth to ask what's going on, but Cirone kicks me under the table and flashes me a warning look.

"What are you talking about?" Rosario waves Carlo off. "Go on, boys, eat. No one's trying to run us out of business. It's just a complaint about goats."

"It starts with goats. Then it grows." Giuseppe gestures angrily with his fork. "Dr. Hodge and men like him— plantation owners, cotton-gin owners. Big bosses. They need straightening out."

I close my fingers tight around my fork. I don't know who's right, but I hate the way Giuseppe's talking.

"Dr. Hodge is no problem," says Francesco. "I know how to talk to him."

"Oh, sure, you and the doctor, you're friends. Bah!" Giuseppe says. "You have a cigar with him—what? once a year?—and you think that's something?"

"It is something! Dr. Hodge doesn't own a plantation— he isn't one of them. He likes us. You leave Dr. Hodge to me. I'll take care of him in the morning."

"You better." Giuseppe jams his fork in the salad. "You just better."

"Eat," says Carlo. "Everybody eat."

I stuff my mouth.

Francesco pushes his empty plate away. He looks at me. "You still thinking about alligators?"

I'm so startled, for a second I can't answer. "A little."

"Vicious!" Rosario makes a monster face, wrinkling his big nose and putting his hands beside his cheeks like threatening claws. Then he laughs. "I saw a giant one roped up in the back of a wagon once. Long like you wouldn't believe. The length of two men standing on top of each other. Still alive. Even when they close their jaws their teeth show." He leans toward Cirone. "As if they're smiling at you and saying, 'Hello, dinner. My, you look tasty.' "

That's exactly what the 'gator head over the saloon looks like it's saying. I grip my fork so tight it hurts. Cirone chews the corner of his thumb.

"Good eating, though," says Francesco. "We had them in New Orleans."

"The figs will be ripe in July," says Carlo. "I can make alligator with fig sauce. In autumn I'll make it with pomegranate sauce. In winter I'll get oranges from a plantation near New Orleans. Sicilians work there—so the fruit is good."

"Figs, pomegranates, oranges." Francesco rests his elbows on the table and takes a loud breath. "They didn't have good fruits or vegetables in this state before the Sicilians. Without us, all they'd eat is squirrel and possum and alligator."

"And chicken," says Carlo. "They eat chicken on Saturday nights."

Francesco gets an odd, sad look on his face. "It smells good, the way they make it. The way they sit outside and laugh together and play music."

"We have fun on Saturday nights, too," says Rosario.

"Yeah," says Giuseppe. "We've got each other. Who needs them?"

six

Cirone and I shift from foot to foot as Francesco inspects the new porch floor. We spent all day building it. He checks the edges to see if they're even. He runs his fingers over the surface to see if we lined up planks of equal thickness to make it level. He grabs ends here and there to see if we put in enough nails so that they won't jiggle.

I jam my hands in my pockets. Cirone does the same. I bet his are balled into fists like mine.

Francesco walks the length, stopping and flexing his knees every few paces. He stamps.

We flinch.

Francesco smiles. "Fine job." He does a dance across the floor. One of the circle dances we do together on a Saturday night.

Cirone and I hoot and hug each other.

"Tomorrow you take the old step that used to be in front of the door and you attach it right here." Francesco taps his foot at the outside edge of the porch across from the door. "Then paint the whole thing white."

"White?" I say. "On a floor?"

Francesco glowers. "What's wrong with white?"

I've got a stake in this porch. Cirone and I spent all day Thursday choosing the planks, lining them up, planing the irregular ones. And today was all sawing and hammering. My back aches and my hands are ripped up. And that's two days in a row I haven't been there to see Patricia walking home from school. She's all I can think about. "Everyone tramps dirt across a porch. White will look bad fast."

Francesco points at Cirone. "And you, what do you think?"

Cirone hardly ever talks in front of the men, and now with Francesco's finger aimed like that, he squirms. "Goats run across porches," he mumbles at last.

In Francesco's eyes the goats do no wrong; I'm flabbergasted at Cirone's daring. So is Francesco—he blinks and pulls on his mustache. It's not a good sign when Francesco does that. But he laughs, and Cirone does, too. I finally join in.

"All right, all right." Francesco rubs his hands together. "You'll paint it black. But later. Tomorrow paint it white. The day following that is Sunday, so I'll invite Dr. Hodge over for *limoncello* after he gets out of his fancy church. He'll say no—they all say no—but I'll insist. He'll see how fancy we can be. With a new wood porch, white and clean. As good as his. We'll have a nice talk. After the doctor goes home, you can paint it black."

Wasting all that white paint—all that money—just to impress the doctor?

Supper is quiet; things have settled down. Francesco's talk with Dr. Hodge yesterday morning went well. Francesco told Carlo all about it, and I eavesdropped. The doctor didn't mention goats. Just like Joe Evans said, he only wanted to talk about Willy Rogers—about both of them not "overreacting." Francesco is going to leave his shotgun at home. And when Willy needs groceries, he'll send a servant. If the two men see each other on the street, one of them will cross to the other side. That's what the doctor promised, anyhow. The shotgun is closed away in Francesco's trunk for the next time someone goes hunting.

We move outside and sit on the floor of the new porch to eat cold berries for dessert. And I'm happy we've got a porch now.

"Strawberries." Carlo holds up his bowl. "And not the small wild ones from the woods—big fat juicy ones."

"All the way from Tangipahoa Parish, down south,"

says Francesco with pride. "Sicilians own practically the whole parish. Fields and fields."

"Imagine a Saturday night down there," says Rosario. "Like heaven—Sicilians dancing and singing."

"And eating." Francesco puts a berry in his mouth and sucks noisily. "Perfect."

And Carlo knew the perfect thing to do with them. He put them in the icebox. They froze and their inner parts got all squishy, so they melt in our mouths.

Five goats come trotting around from behind the house.

"Stay back!" Giuseppe shouts at them.

They stop. Giuseppe's the only one gruff enough to make the goats behave. But Bedda jumps onto the porch and head butts Francesco in the shoulder. He grabs her by the hair at the front of her chest and feeds her a strawberry.

"What are you doing that for?" says Giuseppe in disgust. "Tomorrow is June third. Decoration Day. The whole town will be buying food for parties. These strawberries will sell at top price, every last one of them."

Bedda's baby, Giada, takes a timid step forward. Giuseppe slams the back of his shoe against the porch, and the little thing goes skittering off to the others.

I ask, "What's Decoration Day?"

"A day to honor the men who died in war," says Carlo. "Big celebrations."

"Except the rest of the country celebrated it this past Tuesday," says Giuseppe.

I look at Giuseppe, puzzled.

Francesco leans across Bedda's neck toward me. "Louisiana and some other states in the South—they have their own laws. The rest of America celebrates on May thirtieth and honors men who died on both sides of the Civil War. Here they celebrate on June third, Jefferson Davis' birthday, and honor just the Confederate dead."

I know I've heard Jefferson Davis' name in my lessons with Frank Raymond. "So we're celebrating?"

"Course not." Francesco gives Bedda a kiss between her eyes, then stands and stretches. "This is nonsense—honoring only their own. But on Decoration Day people need food for parties. You boys paint the porch first thing in the morning—white paint. Then hustle over to the grocery store."

"Aw," says Cirone under his breath.

We had planned to paint slowly and take the whole day at it, go a little easy. "Both of us?" I say. "Who'll help Rosario at the stand?"

"I hired two men," says Rosario. "You boys work in the grocery."

Cirone and I exchange doleful glances.

Rosario gets his mandolin and plucks a few notes. "Who wants to sing tonight?"

"Me." Francesco reaches into his pocket. "And here. For you boys." He places pennies on the floor between us: one, two, three, four. Four! "In case you want to skip the music and go have some other kind of fun tonight."

I pocket all four pennies. After all, I'm older. "Thank you."

"Thank you," says Cirone.

We walk toward town, our uncles' songs fading in the background. It will be the usual night at home—music and dance and cigars. Pretending like they're back in Sicily, surrounded by neighbors, joking and laughing. Just the four of them. Or maybe only three, 'cause they take turns going across the river to Vicksburg for fun. Vicksburg is four times the size of Tallulah; there's plenty going on.

All at once I'm blue, thinking about them. They're lonely. At least Francesco is—saying all that to Joe. If I didn't have Cirone, I don't know what I'd do.

"How about the slaughterhouse?" asks Cirone as soon as we're out of sight.

"You want to risk crossing a panther again?"

"Aw, come on. He didn't hurt us."

"Why do you like that place so much, anyway?"

Cirone says real quiet, "My father was a butcher."

My father was a fisherman. With thick arms from pulling in nets, and pocked cheeks from facing the salty wind all the time. He left for America to find his fortune, right after Rocco was born. We never heard from him again. I was ten when I last saw him, but I remember everything about him, his voice, even his smell. Cirone was only four when he last saw his father. What can he possibly remember? "All right. But I'm not going near the woods where that panther came out. Race you."

We run across the meadow, past the lit-up slaughter-house, then I punch Cirone lightly in the shoulder and slow us to a walk. Running in town draws attention. A few minutes later I turn onto Cedar Street.

"Not yet." Cirone catches me by the elbow. "The ice cream saloon isn't for two more blocks."

I smile. We haven't said a word to each other about where we're going to spend those four cents, but of course the ice cream saloon is the best choice. I feel proud at the idea of going somewhere public without my uncles, which is dumb. I'm fourteen! But Francesco keeps tight rein on us, as though we're little kids, so this is new to me.

"If we go down Cedar, we pass the courthouse," I say.

"Who cares? What do you want to look at it for?"

"It's different at night."

"How?"

"Did I give you a hard time about going past the slaughterhouse?"

Cirone pads along after me.

Sometimes I think I'll never get used to the dirt streets here. I miss the cobblestones of Cefalù. But at least the dirt lies flat tonight. In the daytime it's dusty, stirred up by peo-ple, wagons, horses, carts, mules, hogs.

Dead quiet.

Except for the crickets. There must be millions of them.

We pass Sheriff Lucas' house, and his two dogs charge off the porch, ears and jowls flopping. I'm glad there's a fence. The dogs are massive, and their short hair covers loose, wrinkled skin. I pull back. Cirone reaches between pickets and pets one.

I gasp. "Are you crazy?" But that dog is acting as if he likes it.

"They don't bite unless the sheriff tells them to."

I feel stupid. "I thought you didn't like dogs."

"I don't." Cirone shoves the hand that petted the dog in my face.

"Yuck." I sneeze. "That stinks."

Cirone laughs. "Their drool stinks even worse."

A soft sound comes from above. It's a large bird. From the ragged zigzags I know it's a yellow-headed night heron. Francesco taught me that. They're good eating.

The redbrick courthouse looms at the corner of Depot Street, a two-story giant with front balconies and chimneys up the north side. On the south a stand of cottonwoods lifts its arms as if in praise. The windows are tall, and the columns and railings and arches on the balconies seem to move in the dusky light. At the very top a little alcove juts up with a round window, like a loving eye looking out over everything. It seems a grand, welcoming home. The seat of justice. It presides over Tallulah, like the cathedral presides over Cefalù.

Cirone elbows me in the ribs. "Look."

Three boys walk bent, picking things up off the road, throwing them in sacks.

"Hey," I call.

Charles jerks his head up, then away. The other boys don't even bother to look.

I pull on Cirone's arm.

"Stop," he says. "Don't go near them. They hate us."

"What are you talking about?"

"Everyone hates us." Cirone curls his shoulders and shrinks in on himself. "You don't know."

"What? These boys are all right." I drag him over. "What're you doing?" I say in English.

"Y'all ain't got eyes?" Charles doesn't look up.

Stupid question. They're collecting horse manure.

Cirone moves closer to me. "How come?" he says real soft.

I don't get to hear Cirone speak English much. But I know he talks good. He sounds like everyone else from Tallulah, not like Frank Raymond, which is who I sound like. No one accuses Cirone of talking fancy, like Mrs. Rogers said to me.

"What you use on your fields?" asks Rock. "Human turds?"

The boys laugh.

It takes me a second, 'cause that's the first time I've heard that English word, but I'm laughing, too. I'm laughing so hard, I double over. Then I pick up dung. The soft, round ball smells sweet. I drop it in Ben's bag, closest to me.

All three boys straighten up and look at me.

I pick up another piece and add it to Rock's bag. Then Cirone does the same and we're all picking up clods. We go the length of Depot Street, through the town center. Men are noisy in the whisky saloon. Families are noisy in the ice cream saloon. I look through the window. Boys my age are scrambling to buy soda water for girls, offering them gumdrops and peanuts from the candy store. Children sit on laps and eat ice cream from shiny spoons. A man pounds out a quick melody on the old piano.

Whatever they pay the piano player, I'm sure it's more than Patricia gets for cleaning the Baptist church. "Hey, Charles." I walk up beside him. "Hear that? Your sister should apply for a job playing piano."

Charles drops his head toward me. "You sure you smart enough to collect dung?"

"What?"

"Colored folk ain't allowed in that ice cream saloon. We stand outside and put our money in a cup on the ground, and they lay us a scoop on a piece of old newspaper."

My face goes hot. It's those Jim Crow laws again—whites and Negroes can't be served food in the same eating establishment at the same time. How could I forget? But I work all day, every day but Sunday. I go to bed early, except Saturday. I don't really see how this town works.

I wonder what Cirone's thinking as we pass by the laughter of those families around the piano. Can he taste the ice cream we're not eating? I pray he doesn't say it. But he won't. I bet he never forgets who is and isn't allowed in the ice cream saloon or anywhere else. Cirone knows everything. He doesn't even give me a meaningful glance. He just throws dung balls in the boys' sacks.

We own two horses: Granni and Docili. In the winter they stay in the shed. Hired hands muck out the stalls and spread the manure on our fields. That's what any farmer who can afford it does. But I never thought about the farmers who don't have horses. There are farms around here where men push plows through the dirt with their shoulders.

A dog barks; a second joins him.

"Sheriff Lucas' dogs," says Charles. "They'll be a-howling all night."

Goats trot over the railroad tracks and up Elm Street. Five. They're ours. I bet they passed by Sheriff Lucas' and drove those dogs wild. Have they been tramping on Dr. Hodge's porch? I look around anxiously. Will the doctor come tearing after them?

Nothing.

We go on collecting dung. When we reach West Street, at the edge of town, Charles stands straight and presses a hand into the small of his back. In the dark he seems like an old man. The other boys roll their heads around on their necks and swing their arms, like Francesco dancing across the new porch.

Cirone had the same thought, because he throws

himself into the middle and dances the tarantella. He hops around, clapping over his head like a crazy man. Before you know it, all of us are running and hopping and clapping for no reason, but it's so much fun. We dance till we fall exhausted in the grass by the side of the road.

"Some dancer!" Rock says to Cirone.

"So, this mean we taking Dancer 'gator hunting, too?" Charles says to me.

I'd hoped he'd forgotten about that. "I don't know."

"You got a name, Dancer?" Charles says to Cirone.

"Cirone." He holds out his hand to shake.

"That's a dirty hand you got there."

"No dirtier than yours," says Cirone.

Charles laughs and they shake. Then Cirone shakes hands and exchanges names with Rock and Ben, too. But they all keep calling him Dancer.

"You coming 'gator hunting?" asks Rock.

"Are you really going?" Cirone says in Sicilian in my ear.

I look quickly at the boys. I don't want them hearing Sicilian; it reminds them we're foreigners. I want them to be friends. Our first American friends.

But the boys don't seem to care.

"I don't know," I answer in Sicilian. "It's dangerous."

"They do it, and they're still alive." Cirone turns to Rock. "Yeah. When?" He doesn't even notice I haven't agreed.

"School out, so we can go to the swamp anytime," says Charles.

"Monday," says Rock.

"Monday," repeats Ben.

My throat is too tight to speak.

"Where South Street end at Brushy Bayou—meet there. Monday after the midday meal."

"We got to work," I manage to squeak out.

"You think we don't?" says Ben.

"A little time off won't starve no one," says Charles. "You two the food men. So bring food."

"Dago food?" says Ben. "Forget it. I can haul supper in a sack. Breakfast, too."

"Breakfast?" I say in quick alarm. "We're going to stay all night?"

"Bless your soul," says Rock. "Y'all don't know nothing. Night the only way."

seven

My family's sitting out back of the house, the six of us on the kitchen benches that Cirone and I carried out here. We fold our hands and listen to Father May's gospel.

The three Difatta brothers share one bench: Carlo, Giuseppe, and Francesco. From shortest to tallest, fattest to thinnest, oldest to youngest. They look so much alike, it's as though the Lord made them out of the same size lump of clay, but with each version pulled the clay more upward than outward. Even their hair is the same, close-cropped and wavy. I wish I looked more like them.

But I look like my father. And my brother Rocco looks

like me. That's good. How it should be. I blink and try to pay attention to what Father May's saying.

Father May is French, so he's giving the gospel in that language. We don't understand a word. Still, we try to look interested. The rest of the service is a mix of Latin and English. Father May's Latin isn't like the church Latin back in Cefalù, and his English is hard to make out. But the Lord knows we're doing the best we can.

Father May travels to small Catholic groups all around north Louisiana. There isn't a Catholic church to be found anywhere, but Francesco says if you scratch hard enough, you'll always find Catholics anyplace—and anyplace makes a fine setting for a Mass.

I look forward to Father May's visits. I never fail to receive the sacrament of Holy Communion when he makes it to Tallulah. Mamma would be glad about that.

Rosario sits beside me. He whispers, "I like the service outside. And just once a month. Not like in Sicily where the women dragged us to church every week."

I'm surprised his thoughts are so far from mine.

Goats wander through, nibbling at our pant legs. No one pays them any mind. In Sicily goats run free, too, but they aren't allowed in church.

I miss a real church. The cathedral in Cefalù has two bell towers and high ceilings and mosaics. When you kneel under the centerpiece, you know the Lord watches over you, no matter how small you are. I went there every week with Mamma. And she'd let Rocco sit on my lap. She said I was best at keeping him quiet, but I think she didn't want him to wrinkle her Sunday dress. After she died, I took Rocco to Mass myself. But only for three months. Then I left for America.

A pang of homesickness hits me. Is Rocco in church now?

When the service ends, I pump fresh water from the well, and we all wash our hands in front of Father May to impress him with our cleanliness.

We carry the benches inside to eat. I'm silent through it all, because I have little idea what Father May is saying. I think no one does, but they talk anyway, as though it doesn't matter that they're talking past one another. Usually Cirone and I trade glances at this point in Father May's visit, but Cirone is lost in his own world today.

I'm alone. I feel strange, almost chilled.

With my eyes I beg Carlo to excuse me. He's in charge of mealtime.

When he finally gives me the nod, I run like mad for Frank Raymond's. I'm always late to my lessons when Father May's in town.

"I've got questions today," I say as I burst through the door.

"I knew that." Frank Raymond is cleaning the paint out of his brush. He looks at me. "Do you know what a joy it is to paint by this window in the morning?"

I smile. "Morning light is best. You tell me every Sunday."

"This week I've been in the saloon working on that blessèd mural." He sighs. "I've missed this window—this light."

"If you miss painting in your room, why do you call the saloon mural blessèd?"

"Hot meals, my dear Calogero. On the house."

"What about your afternoons? Your experiences?"

He laughs. "All painters need experiences in order to make art. Have I told you that before?"

"A thousand times."

Frank Raymond holds his brush up to the window, then cleans it some more. Maybe he's forgotten I'm here. That same lonely feeling I had at noon dinner washes over me again. I'm the only person Frank Raymond tutors. If it weren't for me, he could have at least Sunday free. Does he wish I'd go away? I'd miss him if he told me to. A lot. I clear my throat to remind him I'm here.

He looks at me, solemn. Then he goes to the table, dips snuff, and turns to me. "So, question number one?"

"How come you talk fancy?"

He grins. "Who says I talk fancy?"

"Mrs. Rogers said I talk fancy—and I talk like you."

"I'm educated."

"How come Mrs. Rogers doesn't talk like us?"

"She never went to school."

"What? How do you know?"

"After the war the federal government said everyone

60

was allowed in the public schools. But the whites refused to send their children to school with the children of their former slaves. For about ten years white children in Louisiana got no education, until they built separate ramshackle schools for the Negroes. It was even longer here in Tallulah. And that's right when Mrs. Rogers would have been school age."

I'm stunned. But that isn't the whole story—it can't be. "I've got friends now. They go to school, but they still talk different from you. And me."

"People from different places in America talk differently." Frank Raymond spits in his little spit cup, then chews his snuff. "Your pronunciation is more and more Louisiana. Southern talk. But at least you still make good Iowa sentences, like me."

I don't want to make good Iowa sentences. I want to talk like my friends, and Cirone. But that's not worth arguing over, since Frank Raymond isn't going to teach me Southern talk. "So, tell me, what's *lynch* mean?"

"I've been thinking about that since I saw you Wednesday morning. You know how I respect words. But *lynch* is one of the ugliest words ever. When a crowd gets it into their head to kill someone, and they do it—that's a lynching."

"Like killing a murderer?"

"The crowd might think someone committed a murder," says Frank Raymond. "Or stole something. They think whatever they want. But, murderer or no murderer, crowds are not supposed to hand out punishments. We have a system of justice. Trials. You get to hear what you're accused of; you get to defend yourself. And everyone is presumed innocent until proven guilty." He shifts his shoulders. "What did your uncle Carlo say about lynching?"

"Five years ago seven people got lynched on Depot Street."

"Anything else?"

"They were Negro."

Frank Raymond nods. "Negroes have been lynched all over the South. Hundreds. Maybe thousands. Killed without trials. Now that's murder, Calogero." He chews his tobacco. "Did your uncle say anything else about lynching?"

"No." I get the feeling he's holding back. "What else should he have said?"

"I thought maybe he was talking about the lynchings in New Orleans."

"New Orleans?"

"Eight years ago. Ask him. I bet he knows more than I do."

"He used to live in New Orleans. All of them did."

"Then I'm sure they know more than me. Ask them."

"All right. Why do people call Sicilians *dagoes*? What's it mean?"

"It's an insult, that's all I know."

"One more question: who was Jefferson Davis?"

"Come on. We talked a lot about the Civil War."

"I forget parts."

Frank Raymond purses his lips and looks out the window. "Jefferson Davis died in 1889," he says at last. "I think December."

"And his birthday was yesterday," I say impatiently. "But who was he?"

"Not a bad man. Born nearby—in Mississippi. Went to West Point, the famous military academy. Then he was a cotton planter. Somehow, he wound up a senator."

"He doesn't sound important enough for the whole state of Louisiana to celebrate his birthday."

"Well, I'm no history teacher. Just your language tutor. Though your English is good now, except for that twang." Frank Raymond goes to the window and rests his forearms on the sill. "So. Eventually, Mr. Jefferson Davis wound up president of the Confederacy."

Now I'm confused. "And he wasn't bad? That's what you said."

"You think everybody in the Confederacy was bad?" Frank Raymond's still leaning out the window, so I can't see his face. But the rise at the end of his question tells me he's baiting me.

I'm not stupid. Something as big as the Confederacy has to have had good people as well as bad. But taking the bait is half the fun. "Yes. Francesco says it's the old Confederacy way of thinking that led to the new voting laws."

Frank Raymond turns. "Are you asking me about the voting laws?"

"I guess."

"No one can vote in Louisiana unless they've been residents for five years and pay the poll tax."

"That doesn't sound so bad."

"There's a third requirement: you have to read English. That alone is enough."

"Enough for what?"

"To knock out Sicilians, even if they've become citizens. Most Negroes, too."

All my uncles except Giuseppe have become American citizens. But they can't read. So with the new law they can't vote. "How can they make a law like that?"

"The justification goes like this: if you can't read, you can't understand the Constitution. And if you don't understand the Constitution, you shouldn't vote."

"People can read you the Constitution. And I could translate for my uncles."

"Exactly." He crosses his arms and leans against the windowsill. "So there's a silent motive."

"They want to keep Sicilians and Negroes from voting," I say slowly.

"There's more of you than there are whites. If you took control, the whole state would change."

"But what about Mr. Rogers? What about the white men like him who didn't go to school after the war? They don't read. How can they vote?"

Frank Raymond walks over to a corner and spits in the brass spittoon this time. "You see the problem. The law knocks out whites, too. Mostly poor ones. But the state leaders want whites to vote. So they added a handy little condition: if your father or grandfather was a registered voter in 1867, then you can vote even if you can't read."

In 1867, two years after the end of the war—just two years after slavery ended. I bet there isn't a Negro in the state whose father or grandfather was a registered voter in 1867. I'm sure there is no Sicilian. "Confederate thinking. That's what Francesco hates. So how can Jefferson Davis not have been bad?"

Frank Raymond smiles. I smile back. We love these debates.

"He made a reputation for himself of treating people fairly," says Frank Raymond. "Black Hawk, the great chieftain, was his prisoner and Davis won his respect."

"What's a chieftain?"

"Don't you know what Indians are? I really am a bad teacher. We're going out." Frank Raymond puts on his shoes and flips through the canvases of paintings, choosing one of a deer in a field. He rolls it up. "Time for experiences. Are your horses free?"

"Everyone gets Sunday off. Even animals."

"Well, I hate to rob them of their one day off, but we can feed them something nice when we get back. We'll talk as we ride and keep our time together an English lesson. Officially."

eight

We ride east toward the river, Frank Raymond on Granni and me on Docili. Frank Raymond talks about the Indians, who lived all across this country once. They were here long before the Europeans.

He cuts off the road, and we wind through trees draped in moss. "Stay behind me from here on. The ground gets soft, so you need to know the way. There's a small swamp south of here."

The trees thicken and the sky grows narrow between them, so when we finally come out at the river, it seems the world is opening up to us, water and sky forever.

The Mississippi River thrills me. Wide and rolling. The first time I saw it, Giuseppe and Cirone and I went to the town of Delta and watched the Vicksburg port from our side of the river. Wagons pulled up at the dock and bales of cotton were loaded onto a steamboat. Steamboats bring millions of bales to New Orleans all the time. Tallulah people say this is cotton land like nowhere else on earth.

But where Frank Raymond and I have come out today, there are no boats. Nothing to look at but the river itself. I've always loved water and swimming. From the hilltop where the cathedral stands in Cefalù, you can watch the sea. This river is different from the sea. No waves, no tides. But it calms me, all the same. The air above the water shimmers alive with spirits. Ghosts—but good ghosts. It makes my soul feel . . . cradled. It's as good as stepping inside any cathedral. I make a promise: when I'm grown, I'm going to live near water.

"For a long time the Mississippi was the dividing line in America." Frank Raymond walks his horse beside mine as we turn north. "Everything civilized happened to the east of it, and no one got too flustered about what happened to the west of it. That's why the government decided to make the Indians move west, across the river. But Black Hawk stood up for his people. He said they didn't want to cross over."

"So there was a war?"

"You understand American history!"

Sicilian history has plenty of invasions in it, I think. "Will I get to meet Black Hawk?"

"Black Hawk's long dead. No, we're going to visit my friend Joseph. I haven't seen him for a month."

The horses pick their way along the bank of the winding river, then we cut inland through grasses, till we come out on a small, still pond with a cluster of purple flowers in the water at the far end. There's a little shack on one side with a stovepipe sticking out the top.

We get off and drop the reins so that the horses can wander, drink, and graze. They won't run off.

The sun is high and hot. I walk to the water and kneel to drink.

"Hana!"

I turn at the strange word.

An old man emerges from the trees with a musket pointed right at me. All I can see is the wavering mouth of that barrel as he approaches.

"Hello, Joseph," says Frank Raymond.

Joseph squints at Frank Raymond and lowers the musket. I can see his face now. Bags under his eyes, hanging jowls, loose earlobes. He looks ancient. His shirt is embroidered with white seed. A necklace of red-and-white-striped beads glints in the sun. And his white hair is held back by a bead band around his forehead.

Joseph sits beside Frank Raymond, not even leaning on anything as he lowers himself. He's agile for someone so old.

"Joseph, this is my friend Calogero."

Joseph nods as I walk up to them.

"A pleasure." The instant I say that, I feel stupid. Americans say *hello,* not *a pleasure.* I'm translating from the Sicilian, 'cause that gun made me so nervous.

"Calogero had never heard of an Indian before today."

Joseph sits taller, his eyes on me. "Now you see the whole tribe. I am Joseph. I am the Tunica tribe."

I sit beside him. "How can you be a whole tribe?"

"A hundred years ago they drove my tribe from the lower basin of the Yazoo River south into Louisiana. Near where the Red River comes closest to the *titik*–the big river–the Mississippi. People there still call themselves Tunica. Maybe fifty of them. But they are mixed breed. I am the only full-blooded Tunica left alive."

"What does *mixed breed* mean?"

"It is your blood. They have names for different blood. If one parent is white, the other Negro, they call you mulatto. If one or both are mixed, they call you griffe or sacatra or quadroon or octoroon, depending on how much Negro blood and how much white blood you have."

"Why? Who cares?"

"The French fools over in Cane River country. They are strict about who can do what–who can eat where, what people can walk ahead of what other people. But with the Indians it is just are you full-blooded, or do you have Negro or white blood in you–then, mixed breed. I am full-blooded Tunica. The only one. I am the Tunica tribe."

"I guess that means I'm full-blooded Sicilian. Not the only one."

"Sicilian?" Joseph shakes his head. "We do not let Sicilians off the boat in Indian ports. You brought the yellow fever."

"We did?" What's yellow fever? I look at Frank Raymond.

"That's just putting blame where they want it to go," says Frank Raymond.

"You sure about that?" asks Joseph.

"Yellow fever breaks out when people are poor and crowded together and dirty and hot and the bugs are biting like mad. It doesn't matter what blood you have. Sicilians didn't bring yellow fever."

"So why would anyone say that?" I ask.

"If you don't want people to like someone, just call him disease infected."

"Lies." Joseph clicks his tongue. "They tell lies about Indians, too. If I had stayed by the Red River, well . . . *yaxci* . . ."

"What's that mean?" I ask.

"I would get angry. I would get sick."

"Which one? Angry or sick?"

"It is one word in Tunica. If you are angry, you are sick. Too much ugly in that part of the world. I would have ended angry and sick; so the Tunica tribe would have ended angry and sick. That is not an honorable ending for

70

an honorable people. I crossed the *titik*–the big river–back to our land, so the tribe could end properly. But Vicksburg people are nosy, and would not leave me alone. I had to cross the great *titik* yet again to find quiet." He looks around. "This is my burial ground."

He's come here to die. I pull my knees to my chest, wrap my arms around them.

Frank Raymond goes over to Granni. He unties the rolled-up canvas from his saddle, and brings it to Joseph.

Joseph inspects the painting, and smiles. "*Ya*–deer. Are you hungry?" He goes into his shack and comes out with two blackish brown squares.

Frank Raymond chews on his. So I try it. Salty and tough and wonderful.

"Dried venison," says Frank Raymond.

Joseph goes into the shack again and comes out with a bundle wrapped in wet cloth. He opens it. It's a large lump of gray clay. He uses a thin sheet of bark to slice off a hunk for Frank Raymond, and another for me, and a third for himself. Then he wraps up the rest and puts it back away in his shack.

Joseph looks at me solemnly. "Every Tunica man knows how to make pottery."

"Every single one?"

"I know how. So it is true." He smiles.

He caught me. I laugh.

"*Wixsa.* Every Tunica man knows how to joke, too."

Joseph and Rosario would like each other.

We pass the afternoon making bowls. Joseph hums, but Frank Raymond talks a blue streak. He explains the clay came from the bottom of a stream. When we add handfuls of grit, he explains it's crushed shells. Clams and mussels.

We press the heels of our hands into the clay, then rock it down and press again. That removes the air bubbles so that the clay won't explode in the fire. We pinch the clay to shape it, pinch and smooth.

Cracks form in my bowl. Joseph gets a wooden bowl from his shack. He lines it with a fine net, sets my bowl in it, and goes back to working his own. I stare. Then I get it. I press my clay into the wooden bowl. The outer bowl gives the inner one shape. Now it's easy to smooth out the cracks.

We wet our bowls and run the blunt, fat-lipped edge of a clam shell over the surface to smooth even more. Joseph eases my clay bowl out of the wooden one. I peel off the net. It leaves a nice crisscross design.

Then we decorate our bowls, using bits of antler to draw with. Frank Raymond hums with Joseph.

I add pear-shaped loops inside the diamonds of my crisscrosses. The loops look like pawpaw fruit. And I hum, too—that song Patricia taught me about picking up paw-paws.

Joseph sets the bowls on a wooden tray with a wet cloth draped on top.

"That's so they can dry slowly," says Frank Raymond. "Then he'll bake them in a pit fire."

I watch Frank Raymond and Joseph, and I understand why they're friends. I understand why someone would go someplace to spend his last days making bowls.

Joseph didn't come here to die, after all. He came to live. In beauty.

nine

Monday night the boys are waiting for us at the end of South Street.

"What'd you tell him?" asks Charles. "The tall one. Frank."

He means Francesco. But I like it that he's made the name sound American. I wish he'd do that to mine and not call me "Mr. Calo-whatever." "I asked if we could go exploring."

"Didn't tell him it was a 'gator hunt?"

I shake my head.

Charles smiles in approval.

"That hairy bear?" says Rock. "He let you go that easy?"

"He belong in Alligator Bayou with them other bears," says Ben.

The skin on my scalp tightens. "The bayou has bears?"

"You scared?" Charles slaps my shoulder lightly. "Don't waste your energy. Bears hide. You need a bloodhound to hunt them down, like what the sheriff have for tracking criminals. We ain't hardly never lucky enough to see them."

"What y'all want to worry about . . . well." Ben turns his back for a second and takes something from his pocket. Then he swirls around and goes, "Ahhh!" His mouth is open wide and full of cotton.

I stare.

Ben takes the cotton out of his mouth and laughs as though he's the most hilarious person in the world.

"Cottonmouth snakes," says Charles. "In the swamps. By the time you see them, you already bit. So you might as well not even look."

"Snakes?" I say weakly.

"Can't swing a cat without hitting one," says Charles.

Rock gives a little shake of his shoulders. "I ain't hardly afeared of nothing 'cept snakes."

"But they better than snapping turtles," says Ben. "A snake will at least kill you fast. But a giant turtle'll take your foot off with a snap, then leave you to get eaten alive by whatever come along next."

Cirone presses up beside me. "Are they pulling our leg?" he asks in Sicilian.

"They must be," I say back in Sicilian. "Only crazy people would go into the swamps if it was that dangerous." But my heart's beating double time.

We walk. The boys keep joking, and I refuse to listen.

We pass a plantation. Rock points. "Them log cabins over there, see them? Slaves lived there before the War Between the States. Colored tenants live there now." He bounces his finger in the air beyond them. "Kitchen house, barn, smokehouse, gristmill, 'nother barn, cotton house, cotton gin, overseer's house, owner's house, blacksmith's shop. And the chapel."

"Just about a complete village," says Ben.

A few tenants of the rich owner are hoeing among the bushy green cotton plants. Right now those plants look like nothing special. When I first got here last October, though, it was the very end of the harvest season and I saw a field with cream white bolls all burst open. It was so pretty.

We pass a rice paddy and more small houses and outbuildings. Then nothing. No buildings. No noise. Just our joking around and the birds and the insects.

We fall silent.

I'm thinking ahead to giant jaws with giant teeth. The

bears and the cottonmouths and the snapping turtles, they might all be a joke. But the 'gator's for real.

Ben's carrying an unlit lantern with one hand and a food satchel slung over his shoulder with the other. The lantern makes a slight squeak when it swings. Soon we're all walking in time to that squeak. Walking and walking. I want to ask how much farther it is, but I don't want to sound like I'm complaining.

"No one lives out here," I say.

"Floods just about every year." Charles waves his arm. "Sometimes two or three times in a season. Who can live in that?"

Slowly we walk through thorns and bushes and trees. I stop. "What are those?"

"Canebrakes," says Charles.

Plants taller than a house stand close together, choking out everything else. Their tops ruffle like feathers in the breeze. They rise thick as a wall and run in both directions, blocking passage for miles.

Rock and Charles pull long, wide knives out of leather sheaths on their backs. Ben sneers at me. "No bush knife?" I don't know what I've done to make him dislike me. "Here. This way y'all can be useful, at least." He hands me the lantern and Cirone the food satchel.

Cirone and I each already carry a bag of food. Pizza. Thick crusts with cheese, bitter greens, raisins, and garlic. Carlo learned how to make it when he lived in New

Orleans, right near a man from Naples. I can't wait to see their faces when they taste it. That will teach them not to call our food "dago food."

So now both our hands are full as we follow the boys, who whack a path through the canes. You can't see more than ten steps ahead. The cut-off canes slap back at us, and their sharp ends poke hard.

And then the canes end, and it's like we've passed through a door into a magic world of gauze-covered, graceful shapes. The air is hazy and heavy with water. I feel like I've entered someone's dream.

"Swamp." Rock moves close. "Cypress."

He points out the red gums, white oaks, glossy palmettos. But it's the cypress my eyes go back to. They rise from the black ooze like giants with big lumpy knees.

"Anyone see it?" Charles looks up.

My eyes follow his. "See what?"

"The bear," says Ben, and he laughs, but everyone keeps looking up.

We walk along this side of the canebrakes through the vines and creepers that hang from the trees, trailing all the way to the water. A bark comes from the top of a tree up ahead. A black squirrel races down the trunk and jumps on something white—old antlers. He sharpens his teeth on them, and gives another harsh bark as we pass.

Something leaps from the brush, plops into the water, and disappears. "Swamp rabbit," says Charles. "Good eating."

A fat, furry creature with a striped tail goes by. "'Coon," says Rock.

Well, I knew that. I've seen raccoon coats and hats in Tallulah.

"Follow him?" asks Charles.

"Yeah," says Ben.

We follow that waddling raccoon through the undergrowth to a muddy flat. The raccoon climbs onto a heap of mashed grasses and sets to digging. We stand completely still. The afternoon has passed, and as the sunlight fades, I strain to see.

The raccoon reaches down through the grasses and pulls up a white oval. An egg? He holds it in both paws. It's bigger than a chicken egg. He bites and rips. Thick yellow gook runs down his paws. He wipes his snout with his tongue and buries it in the egg. He eats another, and another. Then he waddles off.

We walk to the pile of grasses and Ben pulls them aside. "Good one. Must have been a big 'gator."

The nest is a shallow hole brimming with eggs. Maybe a hundred. Is the mother coming back? I look around.

"Anybody bring a empty sack?" asks Charles.

"Let's eat now, so we can use my satchel." Ben's already handing out biscuits.

This biscuit sits in my hand, a heavy lump. Cirone's gobbling his down. I take a bite. Good! There's turkey inside.

We finish and Ben passes around a bottle. It's coffee—
nice and strong.

Ben hands out a second biscuit each. I take a bite. Meat
again, but richer and darker and sweeter. I look at Rock
with a question on my face.

Ben laughs. "Mr. Calo-whatever never ate loggerhead
before."

Charles tilts his head. "Someday, with luck, y'all'll taste
Tricia's turtle soup."

Turtle? Some people back in Sicily eat turtle. I wash it
down with coffee.

Now it's our turn. Cirone is handing out the pizza. I
want to kick him. I should be the one to make the offer—
and get the credit. It was my idea to bring pizza.

Ben takes a bite. "Raisins?" he croaks, as though he's
just eaten rabbit droppings. "Who ever heard of raisins in
something salty?"

"I like it." Rock licks olive oil off his thumb and takes a
big bite. "Different."

No one else says anything. But they finish the pizza.

We load soft, leathery eggs into Ben's empty satchel.

"What'll we do with them?" I ask.

Charles looks at me as though I'm daft. "Eat 'em,
course."

"But what if there's a baby inside? Bones and teeth and
bumpy skin and all?"

"There ain't. This is egg-laying week. All the 'gators all

over Louisiana, they laying their eggs this week. Perfect time to gather them."

And now we're looking up into the trees again. Back to the mysterious searching we were doing before.

"There." Rock points. From a crook about eight feet up hangs a boat, roped in place. "Good old skiff."

Charles and Ben climb the tree, untie the skiff, and lower it down.

It's flat bottomed, lightweight, and big enough to hold all of us and then some. Tied inside are three sturdy poles. A small trunk is attached to the bottom and filled with rope. Charles yanks on the rope, section by section, testing it.

We carry the skiff through mud that sucks at my shoes like a live thing. Only Cirone and I have shoes on; we stumble while the other boys walk on, steady. Finally, the skiff slides onto water. We get in and the skiff sinks into the mud. We have to dig the poles in deep to push us off and free.

Charles stands and poles at the rear.

I reach my hand over and cup the water and bring it to my lips.

Rock slaps my hand away. "Swamp water make you so sick, by the time you stop rolling you be late for Christmas."

It's dusk already, and the treetops look like skeletons, stabbing the gray sky. We pass through a cavern of cypress decorated with moss.

Rock points at a cypress with a cavelike opening in its trunk just above the water level. "After the rains the entrance to that holler will be underwater. A 'gator will claim it for his den."

An owl hoots. Another answers from across the swamp.

I swat at a fly. It takes off with a little chunk of my flesh.

"Think that's bad?" Ben points at the blood on my arm. "Ha! In a couple of months, this air'll be so black with flies, y'all'll think it's night at noontime." He stands up. "My turn." He takes the pole from Charles.

We move slowly through the swamp and everywhere I look, the shadows hold vines that could as easily be snakes. And everything looks the same. There are no landmarks. Or nothing I can make out. I want to ask: how will we know the way back?

The pole sinks in lower now. This water must be deep enough to hold 'gators. What if they're under us? What if they come up from underneath and turn us over? I'm sitting in a tight ball in the center of the skiff. I can't bring my arms in any closer.

It's dark now. Ben pulls in his pole and sits down. He strikes a match. The smell of kerosene stings as the lantern glows bright. Instantly the swamp disappears. All that exists is the circle of lantern light.

"Here." Ben digs into his pocket and holds out a cigarette butt.

"That dirty thing?" says Rock.

"It ain't dirty."

"I saw you pick it up with a lump of horse manure the other night."

"I cleaned it off good."

"Listen to them," Charles says to me. "Two cats in a bag."

Ben shrugs. "All right, Rock, don't smoke it, if you that particular." He lights it with the lantern flame, takes a puff, and passes it.

We all puff and pass, including Rock, till the butt is too short to hold.

Ben throws it in the water. *Fsst,* it's gone.

Rock points. "There."

Ben stands and holds the lantern high.

I can see it now. A single, small, shining yellow ball.

Charles poles us closer.

The yellow ball has a black vertical slit down the center. An eye.

Rock moves to the far end of the skiff and waves his arms.

Don't! I want to shout. I huddle tighter.

The yellow ball stays fixed on the lantern light.

"Good," says Charles. "This one mine."

"It ought to be mine," says Ben. "By rights and all."

"My family got rights, too," says Charles. "'Cause of Tricia."

I don't know what they're talking about.

Charles steps to the center and Ben takes his place at the head, still holding the lantern. The yellow ball follows that lantern as we close in. Charles leans toward me and Cirone. "Be ready to move quick to steady the skiff. It'll trick you how fast it can flip."

I grip the rim of the side hard. Steadying skiffs?

Charles holds on to the side nearest the 'gator as Rock poles us up beside him.

That 'gator is still looking at the light. He doesn't seem to see us at all.

Charles punches the 'gator in the back of the head.

I gasp.

The 'gator bobs a little, but still looks at the light.

"Pretty small," says Charles appraisingly. "Mind if we catch only a small one, Mr. Calo-whatever?"

"No," I whisper.

"What you say? Speak up."

"I don't mind."

Rock makes a lasso out of the rope and throws it in a big circle onto the surface of the water, with that 'gator eye at the center.

"Ready?" Charles takes a spear out of his sack. It's short, and sharp at both ends. He holds it over his head and jumps out of the skiff. Jumps right into the swamp, right onto the 'gator's back! I can't believe it! The skiff slaps side to side in the water and I'm clinging to the rim and screaming inside my head. Charles is dead. We're all dead.

When I can see him again, he's got one arm around the 'gator's neck and Rock's pulling the lasso tight. The animal finally seems to come awake, opens his huge jaws in a roar, and throws his head side to side. Charles jams the spear in his mouth.

The 'gator snaps his jaws shut. The whole spear disappears inside, his head is that big. He throws his entire body side to side now. Rock and Ben pull together on the rope, tightening it around the 'gator's throat. But then they stop and let the rope run through their hands, and I don't know why they're stopping, because the 'gator is still alive. It hurls itself now. It rolls. And Charles clings to its back, arms locked around its neck.

Ben stands with the lantern, moving it, trying to keep Charles in sight. But we don't pole the boat. We don't move to help. We just watch. I can't stand this. I don't want to look, but I have to look.

That fight between Charles and the 'gator goes on forever. They roll, struggle, go under, come up. Every time I catch a glimpse of Charles, he looks worse. A tangle of moss covers him. His eyes are closed, and the side of his head is pressed against the top of the 'gator's head. Then he's gone again, as the animal twists away. Sometimes it seems they must both be drowned, they're underwater so long. But when that 'gator comes up again, there's Charles, stuck like a leech.

Finally, Charles and the 'gator are still. Pinpricks go up my arms and neck.

"He's dead," says Cirone in Sicilian, his voice cracking in sadness. He makes the sign of the cross.

Then Charles lifts his head and smiles, like it's all easy fun, like he's riding on the back of a floating log.

And Ben is laughing and pointing at Cirone.

My eyes go to that 'gator, though. He doesn't move. I wait for the powerful tail to thrash. Charles couldn't have strangled him. No one could be that strong.

Rock poles us close, and Ben puts down the lantern and pulls Charles onto the side rim. Cirone and I reach out to help when *whap!* The skiff flips! We're in the water. All of us. And the skiff is on top of us. It's totally dark. The lantern's gone. The water comes up over my collarbone and I'm standing in soft muck that sucks me down.

"Push," shouts someone.

We're all trying to turn the boat back over. It's not that heavy, how could it be this hard? We're pushing and I feel movement around my ankles. Alive and quick.

Someone screams.

The skiff turns and slaps right side up on the water. We're instantly in moon glow, eerie and quiet.

"Me first. Then do what I say!" Ben shouts.

The skiff rocks violently as I hold on to the rim. Ben must have gotten in from the other side. Someone's still screaming.

"Rock, get in and pull in Charles," barks Ben. "Calo, say where you at."

The boat rocks hard again, but I hold on. And the screaming is right beside me. It's Cirone. Oh, God in Heaven, I've killed Cirone.

"Calo!" shouts Ben. "Where you at?"

"Here," I manage.

"I got you." Ben grabs me under the armpits and pulls hard. I'm in the boat now, lying in the middle beside someone panting hard. Charles. "Cirone!" I call.

"I got him."

The boat lurches at one end; Cirone sloshes in. "My foot," he sobs in English.

"Hold still," says Ben. "Rock, help me. A loggerhead. Small. But it won't let go."

"I still got my knife," says Rock. "I'll kill it."

I scrabble over to the shadowy figures and my arms circle Cirone from behind. He twists around and clings to me.

I feel a spurt of cold liquid on my arm. "What was that?"

"Turtle blood."

"Help me, San Giuseppe," mumbles Cirone in Sicilian. "Don't let me die a miserable death. Spare me and I'll pray to you every day. Please, San Giuseppe, please."

"Whatever you saying, stop," says Ben. "That turtle dead. Can you feel your foot?"

"Hurts like hell," says Cirone in English.

Someone laughs. "Some spirit."

"That foot got mashed," says Rock, "but it ain't even bleeding."

"You got those good shoes to thank," says Ben.

"We all owe thanks," says Rock. "The swamp nearly got us tonight."

We're silent a moment.

"My 'gator!" Charles pushes himself upright, then drops back down limp again.

"Floating away dead. Can't hardly see him. Oh, there." Ben points.

"Really dead?" I ask.

"Dead as a hammer." Rock's right beside me, still holding Cirone's leg.

"How? How did you kill him, Charles?"

Charles is panting too hard to answer.

"The spear worked its way into his brain," says Rock. "Like a charm every time."

"Get him," says Charles in a raspy whisper. "Get my 'gator."

Cirone starts to moan and gulps it back. Maybe he's going to be sick.

"Let's get out of here," I say. "Let's get out while we're still alive."

"Get my 'gator."

"Everybody rock to this side." Ben waves one arm through the misty dark like the wing of a giant owl. "Easy like. No more turning over."

We rock. The skiff moves. We rock more. It moves more.

"Now stop and lean the other way, but don't rock. Just lean."

We lean, and Ben leans out the opposite way. "Got it. I got a pole."

"See the others?" asks Rock.

"No. But one will do. Here, Rock."

Rock stands and takes the pole.

"Move us this way." Ben waves that arm again. "Okay, good. Now, you two—y'all sit tight. No helping. Your helping flipped us last time."

Cirone and I crawl to Charles, pushing the turtle away. His neck is cut halfway through, so the head hangs crazylike. And he isn't small. He's as long as my forearm.

Ben and Rock pull that 'gator and he slides in on a sheet of moss. He's longer than Charles. Must be six feet.

Ben stands in the front of the skiff and stares out. "I lost the lantern."

Rock stands at the rear and stares out over the water. "Must have sunk."

"We got the 'gator," says Charles. "Let's go."

"Not without that lantern." Ben gets on his knees and leans out. He puts both arms in the water and swishes around.

"Don't do that!" says Cirone. "You know what's in that water. Let's go home."

"I can't go without it," says Ben, and the way he says it, I understand: that's someone's lantern.

"Let's go back to where we turned over," I say. "We can feel with the pole."

Rock poles us along, stopping often to swish the pole around the bottom. Ben sets his hands on the rim and looks into the water. Nothing but black there. With the 'gator on board, the skiff rides deep. If anyone makes a sudden move, we'll take in water over the sides. We must all have the same thought; no one moves. No one even speaks. It goes on like this a long time. My wet clothes stiffen. The night has passed.

"Hey," says Rock. "Something here."

Ben crawls to him, slowly. "Hold me around the waist."

Rock holds Ben, and Ben leans his whole upper half into the water.

I want to grab him back. His head's in that water!

He's out! One hand plucks moss from his head, the other holds the lantern. "What you waiting for?" he says to Rock. "You so lazy. If you was a dog, you'd lean against the fence to bark."

"Ha! You ain't worth a milk bucket under a bull." Rock poles us steady.

The air turns rosy, and I can smell dawn coming. My eyes meet Charles'.

He lifts his chin toward me. "Glad you came?"

I don't trust myself to answer. I can't let myself think

about what could have happened. "That 'gator," I breathe, holding myself far from it, "he's not a small one."

"Sure he is. See the yellow bands on his tail? A young-un. They grow twice that long, easy. Some grow three times that."

I can't pull my eyes away. The 'gator's back is all spiked, like armor. Two rows of scales stick up along the sides of his tail. His hind feet are webbed. That head that was huge when he opened his jaws in the water is now flat and empty.

I've never even dreamed of anything worse.

"'Gator hide bring sixty cents a foot." Rock shakes moss off the pole.

"And the oil bring forty cents a gallon," says Ben. "All in the tail and the tongue. I bet we get two gallons out of this one."

"Money, money, money." Charles pushes himself up on his elbows. "Ain't you boys got nothing else on y'all's minds?"

"The moss on Charles, now," says Ben, "enough of that to dry out and send to New Orleans to make buggy cushions. Four and a half cents per pound, I hear."

They laugh. Cirone is still cradling his foot in both hands, but he laughs. The idiots. And they're right. That horror—and now we're safe. Oh yeah, I'm laughing—I'm laughing and laughing.

"As for your portion," says Charles, looking at me, "a

'gator supper. Tricia promised to make your portion special good."

"Supper? We didn't earn it." I search for the words. "And we made the skiff flip."

"It ain't over," says Ben. "We got to make a palmetto sled and drag it home. And guess who doing most of the dragging."

ten

Our house sits on open land. Cirone and I have no choice but to walk across the grasses in plain view. It's full morning now; we could have made it back from the swamp a lot faster if Cirone hadn't been limping.

Cirone makes the sign of the cross.

"Who are you praying to?"

"Santa Dimpna."

"Why?"

"I'm asking her to make them still be sleeping."

"That won't help." Mamma talked about the saints all

the time. I know. "All Santa Dimpna does is stop sleep-walking."

"Do you know which saint makes people sleep?"

"There probably isn't one."

"Well, then, I'm praying to Santa Dimpna."

I make a little prayer, too: please, please, let my uncles be in bed.

Francesco stands on the porch, his arms crossed at the chest, his head drooping. He looks like he's asleep on his feet. His head jerks up as we come near. "Where?" His voice is low, quiet, and tired. "Where have you been?"

"I'm sorry," I say.

"Me too," says Cirone.

"Where?"

"With friends," I say.

"Friends? You have friends? Where with friends?"

Nothing I say will sound good. I look down.

"Your shoes are soaking—and don't go thinking you're getting another pair before the year's up, either. Clothes damp, too." Francesco walks around us, inspecting. He picks the last bits of moss off our hair. "Lost your hats. You'll have to dig into the basket where we keep old caps. Where were you?" His tone threatens.

"I'm sorry," says Cirone.

If we don't talk, Francesco will never know.

"You said exploring." Francesco pulls the tips of his mustache. "That means a walk in the woods—home within an hour. Instead, this! If you were doing anything bad, if you were on property you shouldn't have been on, if the sheriff comes telling me . . ."

"We were in the swamps," says Cirone quickly. "No one's property."

"The swamps at night?" Francesco's voice rises. His face goes ruddy.

Cirone's done the damage. "We were in a boat," I say.

Rosario comes running out. "Ah! I thought I heard you." He hugs Cirone and reaches out to tousle my hair, too. "At last. Where were you?"

"With cottonmouths," says Francesco. "In the swamps."

"The swamps!" Rosario pushes Cirone away to hold him at arm's length. "Do you know how dangerous that is?"

"We didn't see snakes," says Cirone.

"Oh, you didn't, did you?" shouts Rosario in Cirone's face. "You don't see these things at night. They see you!"

Carlo and Giuseppe come out on the porch.

"I suppose you didn't see snakes, either," says Francesco to me.

I stare at the ground again. In my head, I will Cirone to stare down, too.

"Speak to me," says Francesco. "Speak or you'll be even sorrier."

"We saw alligators," says Cirone.

"You went to the swamp at night to see alligators?" says Rosario. "Are you blockheads?"

"We hunted one. We killed one," says Cirone. "And we killed a turtle, too." He sounds proud of himself, the little liar. He's nuts to run off at the mouth like that. If he tells his foot is hurt, we're done for.

Francesco shakes his head. "You were off in the swamps with guns?"

"Just a spear," says Cirone.

Francesco looks sick. "You faced an alligator with a spear?"

"Sicilians don't go in swamps." Rosario still has Cirone by the shoulders and he shakes him now. "Sicilians don't hunt alligators."

"We didn't," says Cirone. "Our friends did."

"Who are these friends?" asks Francesco.

Even Cirone can't be stupid enough not to recognize the threat in that question. I move closer.

"This is your doing, Calogero. You're the older one." Rosario shakes a fist at me. "You don't care if you die? All right, that's your business. But you could have gotten Cirone killed." He turns to Francesco. "Are you going to whip them?"

"I'll do it." Giuseppe takes a step forward. "You're not tough enough with these boys." Anger steels his voice. "I'll whip them till they can't walk."

"Do that and they can't work," says Carlo quietly.

"I'll teach them," says Francesco.

"No, I'll whip them," says Giuseppe.

"Listen to Carlo," says Francesco. "We need them to work. Leave it to me, Giuseppe, I'll teach them good."

"You better." Giuseppe slaps his hands as though he's wiping them off. "I'm hungry. Can we finally eat?" He goes inside.

Carlo follows.

Rosario waits, his eyes on Francesco.

"Work," says Francesco. "You will work. All the time. No friends. Work."

"Work? That's punishment?" says Rosario. "Calogero could have gotten my little brother killed."

"Hard work. For as long as I say."

Rosario gives a *harumph,* but he goes inside.

I can't believe how easy we've gotten off. We walk for the door.

"Are you limping, Cirone?" Francesco says.

Cirone shakes his head. He walks normal to prove it.

We go inside and start to crawl into bed.

Francesco follows and catches my arm. "Work." He points at Cirone. "You too."

We've been up all night. I can hardly keep my eyes open. "Now?"

"You heard me."

We eat.

We go to work; Cirone at the stand, me at the grocery. I stock shelves, fill orders. The hours drag. Whenever I doze off, Francesco gives me a hard pinch.

By evening my eyes feel like they've been rubbed in sand. My whole body is sore from dragging the sled with that 'gator. My arm is bruised where Francesco's been pinching me. I stumble home. Supper is a haze. I don't even know what I'm eating.

Francesco, Giuseppe, and Rosario go out on the front porch to smoke cigars.

I stand up from the table and sway; my body is so heavy. Cirone stays slumped over the table. I pull on his arm.

Cirone stands and plods across the room toward the bedroom, weaving. He falls over a pot of goat-milk curds. Stinky white spills everywhere.

Carlo shakes his head. Those curds were set out to cool, to make cheese. If he shouts, the others will come back in, and then who knows what will happen.

But Carlo only takes Cirone by the arm and leads him to bed. Then he does the same to me. He whispers, "What happened to the alligator?"

"He died."

"The meat. What happened to the meat?"

"They took it."

"How stupid can you be? You risk your life and you come home empty-handed?" Carlo shakes his head. "It's just as well. Sicilians don't hunt alligators. Don't do it again. Ever."

I won't. I never want to stare at a yellow-ball eye again.

In my dreams glowing yellow balls surround the boat. Charles jumps onto a big 'gator's back. Other 'gators jump on Charles. The thrashing mass disappears under black water. I wake in a sweat. Snores come from other beds. I drop back asleep.

In my dreams we're in the water, the skiff upside down on top of us. I can't find Cirone; I can't hear him, can't feel him. Cirone! I wake in a sweat and lie trembling.

That swamp is a live thing with an empty heart that beats anyway. No mercy, no mercy, no mercy, no mercy—drumming till you lose your mind. How can Ben and Charles and Rock face it over and over? I roll on my side and Cirone's heels hit my chest. He's curled in an *S*. Somehow, he's asleep. That's good, at least. We're lucky we can use our uncles as an excuse never to 'gator hunt again. I close my hands around Cirone's ankles. I'm the older one. "I'm sorry, Cirone," I whisper. After a while I drop back asleep.

"Get up!" Francesco drags me from bed. I fall on the floor.

The room is half dark. "It isn't even morning."

"Joe Evans is here. You're going out to the fields today."

"What about the grocery?"

"Cirone will help me in the grocery."

"What about the stand?"

"Rosario will manage."

"Please, Francesco."

"You're the older one. You get more punishment. Go with Joe. Now."

I spend the day with Joe Evans and his crew, harvesting lettuce, plowing the roots under, and planting again. By Wednesday evening I'm dead on my feet.

It's the same story Thursday. Friday. Saturday. I have never looked forward to a Sunday as much as this one. The Lord was right when He declared a day of rest.

On Sunday Francesco pulls me out of bed again.

"It's Sunday," I say. "No fair."

"I'm the one who should say no fair. It's my Sunday, too. My only mistake was taking you into this house. I can't sleep late on a Sunday because I have to punish you."

"The grocery is closed. The field hands are at home. How can I work?"

"Plenty for you to do around here. Work I've been putting off. Start with cutting firewood for winter."

"It's June!"

"Get up."

"What about Frank Raymond?"

"You already speak English good enough."

"But he needs the food I trade or he'll starve." That's not the truth, now that Frank Raymond's painting the mural in the saloon. But Francesco doesn't know that.

"I'll give him greens."

"He won't take charity."

Francesco lowers his brows. "I understand that. A man who has to bow too low never gets up again." He looks at me. "All right. Chop wood in the morning. Study in the afternoon. Then you come home and work."

"Thank you."

"I'll walk you there. I'll walk you back."

And so it goes. Day after day. And I've only caught one glimpse of Patricia since that Wednesday—the last day of May. I was carrying crates into the grocery and she waved from across the street. That's all. Not even words, just a wave.

I never want to hear about alligators again in my life.

eleven

I start up from my bed in a sweat. The rooster's crowing. It's already morning. Francesco didn't wake me before dawn. What's going on? When my heart slows, I can feel the hollow pit in my stomach; I haven't talked to Patricia for the entire month of June. I haven't even seen her at a distance but twice.

I turn my head and my nose hits Cirone's toes. He's still in bed, too.

So where's Francesco?

I jump up and wake Cirone. We wash, dress, and eat

the bread and jam waiting for us under a cloth on the table. Carlo's gone. But I know he's close by, 'cause he left everything out. A mound of spinach and wild greens sits on the cutting board. And a bowl full of grated cheese that smells so sharp my nose prickles. A pile of chunks of peppered lard, a pile of diced dried meat. Under another cloth, pie crusts. Lots of them. It makes no sense. Cirone and I each steal a chunk of meat.

He runs to the stand. I run to the grocery. Half the vegetables are already stacked in neat piles in the bins. I take over the rest of the job while Francesco stays busy in the storage room at the rear. He comes out only when the first customer arrives. For the next couple of hours, Francesco and I move around each other peacefully, serving customers as if everything is like it used to be. He doesn't bark orders; I do my job with a smile.

"Hey, Mr. Calo-whatever." Charles comes into the store.

I grin. It's been so long. But no! I've got to get him out of here fast.

Francesco rushes in from the storage room.

"Morning, sir," says Charles. He touches his hat in respect.

I step between them, hands open, trying to think up some excuse for why Charles is here before Francesco explodes in anger.

But Francesco is beaming. "Everything ready." He rubs

his hands together, speaking his big, bold English. "On wagon, out back. Calogero, you go help Charles. You make sure he got everything he need. Everything."

I look from Francesco to Charles and back.

"You no hear? Get going. You drive the wagon, you help unload."

I blink, dumbfounded.

He points at me, that finger that's always telling me what to do. "You ears no work, Calogero? You drive the wagon to church. With Charles. Now go."

Church. He's got to mean Patricia's church. That's the only church Charles would go to. I nod.

"And, Calogero, if they need, you stay." Francesco puts his hands on his hips. "No be lazy. You stay and you make useful."

You bet I'll stay. If Patricia is there, I'll stay all day.

The wagon is waiting out back, hitched up to Granni. I rub the horse's muzzle while Charles climbs in back and checks the boxes.

"All here, I reckon." He jumps off and comes around to the front bench.

I get on beside him and take the reins and we're rolling that wagon slowly out to Depot Street. "What's going on?"

Charles punches my shoulder. "He didn't tell you. I knew it. I knew from the way you acted." He laughs. "You thought the only reason we went 'gator hunting was to show you and Dancer how?" His voice pokes fun. "You did, didn't you?"

I'm no fool. "You did it to make tons of money."

"Ah, we sold that hide," says Charles. "Slit it down the back and emptied it out careful, so the belly skin stayed perfect. Sold the oil, too. But not an ounce of meat went in the cargo for the French market down in New Orleans. Not one ounce." He waits.

This is like with Frank Raymond. Feels like everyone's always waiting around for me to take the bait. Oh, all right. "So what did you do with all that 'gator meat?"

"We got mouths to feed." He's smiling, still poking fun.

"You needed all that meat?" I ask.

"Mmm-mm. Every single bite."

"You must have a lot of mouths at home."

Charles takes off his cap. His hair has been cut really short. There are nicks in his scalp from the clippers. "Ain't never seen nobody look so dandy, right? We having a party. Tonight."

"And the stuff in this wagon is for the party?"

"Every single bite," says Charles. "A graduation party. Seven people graduated from lower school and two from upper school."

"Patricia's graduation!" I practically shout.

"Ben's, too. Seven at once, and two more—two!—made it all the way through upper school." Charles wags his head. "Can you believe it? My uncles already cooking our 'gator in an outdoor pit."

"Our 'gator? You didn't eat it yet? It must be rotten by now."

He laughs. "We smoked it. That make it last. The sauce will be special. We invited every colored family in and around Tallulah. Over a hundred folks will come. Maybe two hundred. Going to be some show. And my family, we running it."

"Wow."

"Uncle Paul and I went over to your place last night to talk about trading for food. You was already asleep in bed, by the way." He bumps me with his shoulder. "My uncle and your uncle, they conversated for a hour. Laughing and drinking. And in the end y'all coming, too."

"My family?" I give a whoop.

We pull up to the church, and a man helps us unload. "This here's Uncle Bill."

Not much later I'm standing in the kitchen porch beside the last box from the wagon, watching the women chop kale, cardoon, chicory. I've kept my eyes open since I got here, but I haven't caught a glimpse of Patricia. Slowly I take celery out of the box and pile the stalks onto a table. Maybe if I hang around awhile, she'll turn up.

I step close to one of the women. "Could I make myself useful, ma'am?"

The women hush and look at me, as though I've said a bad word. Then the one I addressed smiles wryly. "You already been useful, child. And polite. Much obliged."

"So that's where you at." Charles comes in. "Want to see my classroom?"

I follow him down to the basement. Each of the two rooms has a long center table with side benches. I wonder where Patricia sits.

Shelves line the inner walls. Some hold stacks of writing slates. Others have paper tablets. And books! Frank Raymond and I read his newspaper together. But he doesn't own books. I walk along, scanning titles. Copies of the Bible. *Hilliard's First Reader. Hilliard's Second Reader. Cowley's Speller. The New York Speller.* And there's that playwright that Patricia told me about: William Shakespeare.

Patricia's probably held all these books. I pick one up.

"I just finished second year of upper," says Charles. "I'm good in my books."

I think of Patricia saying she's not going on to upper school in autumn. She's going to get her working papers. Why can't she be the one to go on in school? "Doesn't your family need you to work?"

Charles looks at me. "I work all summer. All day long. And I don't stop when school start. I get up and milk the same seventeen cows of Mr. Ralph Burton every morning before school. In autumn I go to Mr. Coleman and chop ten rows of cotton before school and come home to chop another twenty. You ain't the only one who work, Mr. Calo-whatever. Maybe surrounded by fruits and vegetables all day, you think food is everything. Geography and history and music and composition and declamation and 'rithmetic. I care about all that."

So do I. But I don't want to argue. I search for something to say. "Today's July first. How come you didn't have this graduation weeks ago, when school ended?"

"This ain't the ceremony. We had a graduation ceremony, with our teacher and all, the last day of school. This is a celebration for families—proud of us young-uns for getting an education." He puffs out his chest.

I ride the wagon to the grocery. The empty boxes bump around in back.

Francesco greets me with a smile. "A party. And we're invited. You made us friends. That's what we've been missing. Friends and women. You can buy women in Vicksburg, but you can't buy friends. No amount of my offering cigars and drinks has made us friends. The Negroes here are so much more timid than the ones in New Orleans. They just won't take your hand, no matter how far out you stretch it. But you, you changed all that, Calogero. You made friends just selling fruits." He stops. "Ah! Alligator friends?"

I swallow.

He puts up a hand. He drops his head and walks in a circle with that hand still held high. "You are never going in a swamp again! Never!"

"Never." I would stake my life on that promise.

"Never!" he shouts.

"Never." My word is a stone.

He finally stops circling and drops his hand. "Then we understand each other. There are other things to do with friends. Safe things. And that's that." His voice calms and his face changes back to normal. He takes a deep breath. "I like that Uncle Paul. He's all right. And it makes sense we should go to a party at that school. That's supposed to be our school. Sheriff Lucas said so. We'll stay outside where the dancing and singing are. We won't go in the Protestant church part. Just the school grounds." He smiles and shakes his head as if in disbelief. "A party!" He dances between two rows of bins. "You should see what Carlo's making to bring."

"Pasticcia rustica," I say, remembering the ingredients on the table this morning.

"Those pies are so good, they'll be like a present."

A present! "I want to get Patricia a present." The words blurt from me on their own. I don't even know if people give graduation presents here.

"Who's Patricia?"

"She's graduating. It's her party. Charles is her brother. Paul from last night is her uncle." The words keep tumbling out. Would she even want a present from me?

Francesco bobs his head. "Graduating, huh? She needs a nice present."

And in this instant I know exactly the right one. I made it for her—I just didn't know that when I was doing it. "I've got to go see Frank Raymond. About the present."

Francesco rubs his lips. "You're the reason we're invited. So, all right. You go to Frank Raymond's. Then you come back early."

"I promise."

But at that moment the girl who works for Mrs. Severe comes in. I smile. Then I blink. I'd nearly forgotten about the feud. The Severe family is friends with the Rogers family, everyone knows that. So if Mrs. Rogers is boycotting Francesco's grocery, I would have expected Mrs. Severe to do the same. Francesco rushes past me to serve her.

Coming through that door a second later is Joe Evans' wife. Francesco shoots me a look: take care of her fast. I greet Mrs. Evans and run around filling her order. Then Richie comes in. He's been our hired hand on many occasions. Francesco's still serving Mrs. Severe's girl and I'm still serving Mrs. Evans. So I wave to Richie, to let him know I saw him.

Mr. Coleman comes in the door. I feel almost dizzy: four customers at once! He calls out, "What I got to do to get some service around here?"

Francesco is already wrapping the last of the order for Mrs. Severe's girl. He tucks it into her basket and she scurries out, head down.

"Mr. Coleman," calls Francesco. "I be there. I take care Richie, and you next."

"What? You joking? I need them fat strawberries—like you sold us last week."

"Richie here first. You next." Francesco turns to Richie. "What you want?"

Mr. Coleman looks like he's been hit on the head. He points at me. "Boy, get me them strawberries."

I'm wrapping beans in newsprint for Mrs. Evans. My breath catches.

"Now!" he shouts.

Mrs. Evans grabs the beans. "I reckon I have what I need, Calogero. Much obliged." She practically runs out the door.

Francesco is talking friendly to Richie. He doesn't even look at Mr. Coleman.

"Yes, sir!" I say to Mr. Coleman. "Strawberries. They came fresh this morning."

Mr. Coleman's hands are jammed in his pockets. He rocks back on his heels and surveys the ceiling.

"Is this enough?" I hold out a sheet of newsprint piled high with the best berries.

"You say *sir* to me."

"Yes, sir."

"Don't look me in the face. Look at the ground when you talk to a gentleman."

I look down. "Yes, sir. Would you need anything else, sir?"

"Be polite. Not like that crazy man you work for. Serving darkies ahead of whites! Ain't you got eyes? I walk in here and I see three darkies. That makes me first. You got that?" He takes off his cap and smacks it against a bin. "No wonder you people get in trouble all the time. They say you're instigators. But they're wrong. Fact is, you ain't got no sense." He slaps his cap back on, pulls it down hard. "I ain't soft, like Willy Rogers. You ever treat me this way again and y'all won't have no business no more."

I'm shaking now. Polite. That's the second time I've heard that word this morning. Be polite. No matter what. I wrap the strawberries. Perfect Sicilian-grown strawberries, if he only knew—ha! "Six cents, sir."

Mr. Coleman throws the coins on the floor. "I see how y'all give food to them darkies for free. You didn't take a cent from that woman. Not one red cent. Then you over-charge the whites. Y'all're planning something, all right. You pee down my back and tell me it's raining, and you think I don't know no better. Criminals. A bunch of crimi-nals. Willy Rogers got that down, all right." He grabs the strawberries and leaves.

Francesco pats Richie on the back and leads him to the door.

And we're alone. Finally.

"Criminals," says Francesco in Sicilian. "He's the crimi-nal. You and me, we never commit crimes."

"I don't know about that," I say, my voice trembling. "I charged him six cents for five cents' worth of strawberries."

"You didn't! Really?"

"A penny fine. Rudeness."

Francesco comes over and hugs me. "You've got a good head." He laughs.

But I'm fighting tears. "I hate Mr. Coleman."

"You hate him, or you're afraid of him?"

"Both."

"He's not going to hurt us. I won't let him." Francesco chucks me under the chin. "You've got a present to take care of, right? For a friend. Go on, get out of here."

twelve

Frank Raymond isn't in the saloon or in his room over Blander's barbershop. He must be out having experiences—it's almost noon, after all.

I go in the pharmacy and stand on the courthouse porch to peek in those tall windows. I check every store, the post office, the telegraph window. No luck.

So I head out alone, on Granni, riding east toward the Mississippi River. I have a cap on and I bend my head, but the sun beats down so hard, sweat stings my eyes and soaks my shirt. I'm panting.

I didn't ask Francesco if I could take Granni. But I'll have the horse back long before evening. I trot slightly northward; Frank Raymond warned about a swamp to the south.

I don't pass a soul. In Sicily we stay inside in this kind of heat, too. But there this kind of heat happens only in August when the Scirocco wind blows from Africa. Yesterday afternoon Cirone read the thermometer outside the train depot. Over ninety degrees. And he said it'll be like that for months.

We come out on the river at last and the sun on the water blinds me. Granni goes slower. His back is so lathered, I slide side to side in time to his gait. I didn't take the time to saddle him up—it would have only made him hotter, anyway.

We wander up the riverbank, looking for the little meadow where Frank Raymond turned last time. It can't be that hard to find Joseph.

I'm thirsty and Granni sure needs a break from the sun. We stop in the shade of a smooth-barked tree. White petals rimmed with brown litter the ground. The smell is so sweet, it feels damp. As Granni and I drink from the river, we startle a lone pelican, who flaps clear across to the other side of the river.

I feel lost. I should have sat outside Frank Raymond's and waited. A party can sure make a person act foolish. The last big party I went to was my little brother Rocco's baptismal celebration.

Oh! What day is it? Saturday, July first. Rocco's birthday was two days ago. He's five. I didn't even send him a birthday letter and I'm his family, his whole family.

I'll write one tomorrow.

I hope someone celebrated his birthday. Rocco probably doesn't even know the date. And if he does, he's so little he probably doesn't know enough to tell anyone.

He didn't get presents. Well, I'll buy him something Monday. I still have the four cents Francesco gave Cirone and me. I'll have to do something for Cirone to pay him back for his half.

Ferns grow thick near the bank. I break off a pile. I don't have rope, but the ferns bend easy. I tie their stems together and make two mats. One goes over Granni's head and neck, leaving his eyes free. The other drapes over my head and shoulders. Not much, but they'll help against the sun.

I walk with Granni trailing behind. I turn inland through hickory and pine and come out at Joseph's shack. No one is there. But logs poke up into a cone shape from a pit near one end of the little pond. The wood is charred. I walk toward it.

"Hana!" Something whizzes past my nose.

I stumble. My leaf hood goes flying. Granni whinnies and takes off.

Joseph comes into the open, holding a bow with a fresh arrow at the ready, eyes squinted. Then he lowers it. "My friend. I am sorry, friend."

I sink to my knees in relief.

Joseph pulls me up by the arm. "You disguised your head. You disguised your horse. You look like someone up to no good. You are stupid."

And I'm laughing like a drunk man. "You could have killed me."

"It was a warning. Did it come too close? My eyes grow poor. Lucky for you I do not carry my gun today."

"Your gun!" I slap my hand on my forehead. "Your gun, your gun." Tears roll down my cheeks, but I'm still laughing. I fall to my knees, this time with my hands in prayer. "Thank you, San Cristofero," I say in Sicilian.

Joseph pulls me up again. "Do you have weak knees?"

I laugh again and shake my head. "I thanked a saint for making you not carry your gun today. He protects travelers."

"Does your saint steal bullets?"

"No."

"Then you can thank him if you want. It is good to give thanks. But he does not deserve it. I do not carry my gun because I am out of bullets. Bullets cost money. I can make arrows for free. Come catch your horse."

We find Granni and calm him down.

"You came at the right time," Joseph says after I explain why I'm here. "I fire pottery when the moon is full. Last week the moon was full."

I want to ask where my pot is, but it feels rude to rush.

Joseph offers me berries and some kind of mash. "Rest from the heat." He sits under a tree and weaves pine needles.

"What are you making?"

"An alligator basket."

I shiver.

Joseph blinks at me. "You do not like alligator?"

"Who does?"

"He can be ugly. He can be dangerous. But he is honest. He is who he is. You treat him with respect if you want a free life."

What's he talking about? I'm getting the jitters. I watch him weave. A basket could be a birthday present for Rocco. I gather an armload of needles and sit beside him. "Will you teach me?"

"Children and women weave baskets," says Joseph. "Not you."

"You're a man, and you're weaving a basket."

"I am the Tunica tribe. The Tunica tribe weaves baskets."

"I am Sicilian," I say. "There are six of us in Tallulah. My uncles and a cousin. And two in Milliken's Bend. No women or children. I am not the whole tribe. But Sicilians weave baskets."

Joseph looks at me with new interest. "You are an orphan?"

I'm taken aback. "No." Then I falter. "I don't know. My

mother died last summer, and my father came to America years ago. We never heard from him again."

"You are alone in the world."

"No. I have a brother in Sicily. As soon as he's old enough, I'm sending the money for him to come over, too."

Joseph scratches his chest. "You cannot weave. But since you are an orphan, you can listen. The Tunica tribe is good to orphans."

I don't want him calling me that. But if he's decided I'm an orphan, it doesn't matter what I say. I scooch across the ground and rest my back against the base of the tree. And Joseph tells me a story.

The Tunica people lived in a mountain with two alligators outside the entrance. They wanted to come out into the world because they'd been in that mountain since the beginning of time. But the alligators wouldn't move, and they were afraid. So they fasted and said prayers to all nine gods. To the sun, the thunder, and fire—the three most powerful ones. And to the gods of the north, west, south, east, the earth below, and the heaven above. It worked; the alligators slunk aside. One was red and the other was blue. When the red one turned over, the world got hot. When the blue one turned over, the world got cold.

"That is how the Tunica people entered the world and found seasons," Joseph says. He pauses, but only briefly. He tells of beans and corn and floods. He warns against killing frogs (because the world will dry up) and killing kingfishers (because a storm will come ruin you). His voice grows creaky as he talks of the tricks the rabbit plays on everyone, even the gods.

I'm Catholic, so I know the world is full of miracles and mysteries, but I don't believe that at night animals turn into talking people and alligators have mystical powers.

Still, there's something about Joseph's storytelling that catches me. I'd like to stay and listen except it's getting late. "I have to hurry."

"I know. Your face tells me." He doesn't get up, though.

Joseph reads my face. But I can't read his. He never even cracks a smile except at his own jokes.

"One more story. You choose."

I don't have any idea what his stories might be; how can I choose? I think of the stories Frank Raymond told me about famous Indians. And it hits me. "Why are you named Joseph? That doesn't sound Indian."

"An ugly story. I was born Uruna—bullfrog. Boys found out what my name meant. They were not Tunica, not mixed blood. They made me jump, because bullfrog jumps. They made me jump and jump and jump. My feet bled. I fell down. They threw rocks on me. Rocks buried me. My mother dug me out. When I was well enough to walk again, we moved to another town. I became Joseph. A Christian name was safer."

Buried alive! I want to hit someone. I breathe in. Deep. "Why didn't you change your name back to Uruna when you came here?"

"I am Joseph. I remember Uruna. But I am Joseph." He stands and stretches, and carries his basket back to the shack. Then he brings my pot out. It's covered with ashes. He gets on all fours and blows the ashes off. I join him.

The bowl is smaller than I remembered it. And the designs on the outside aren't as distinct. But it will look pretty once I've painted it.

We wrap it in ferns and I thank Joseph.

"Pay attention," says Joseph. "And you can ascend to the sky and become thunder. You can be the manager of the clouds and the rain."

I shake my head in apology. "I don't know what you're talking about."

"An orphan is free to become anything. The choice is yours."

I ride away on Granni, clutching the ash gray bowl to my chest. I don't know what time it is, but I know I'm in trouble. Granni won't speed up. And I don't have the heart to kick him in this heat. It's dusk by the time I reach Tallulah.

Frank Raymond still isn't in his room. I was hoping he'd help me paint the bowl.

I ride toward home chanting inside my head, "It's all right."

They're lined up on the porch. Even Cirone.

I lead Granni out to the field, take off his bridle, and rush back.

Francesco glowers at me. "You promised."

"I promised to be back early, and it isn't dark yet." I hold up the fern-wrapped bowl and put on a sorry face.

"You took Granni without permission," says Francesco. "What's wrong with you? Is your head empty? Get inside."

I walk into the kitchen and put the bundle on the table.

"That present better have been worth it," Francesco says.

I hope so. But now everything feels different. The bowl is dirty gray. And it stinks of ash. Joseph said I was stupid today. He's right.

Cirone comes over and pushes some of the ferns away. "You made that?"

I nod. My eyes burn.

He unwraps it, and turns it over carefully. "She's going to love it."

thirteen

The last time I saw this many people in one place was when my steamship arrived in New Orleans; passengers jammed the top deck of the ship, people swarmed the docks. But that was different, because everyone was going about their own business. Here, everyone has the same business—this giant party. The six of us stand and stare. Charles wasn't exaggerating; there're probably two hundred people here.

"Help me carry the *pasticcia rustica*," says Carlo.

Good old Carlo. We're bringing food; that means we belong here, even if we can't see a soul we know.

We parade back and forth from the wagon to the long line of tables, carrying pies. The tables are already laden with food. We slide a pie in here, another in there.

But now we're empty-handed again. And still surrounded by strangers. They talk and laugh, just not with us. In fact, they give us sideways glances, as though we make them anxious. I avoid their eyes and search for Patricia.

"Look how happy they are," says Francesco. "So easy."

"Bet this is what it's like in Tangipahoa Parish," says Rosario wistfully.

"Yeah," says Giuseppe. "We should be with Sicilians."

"Well, we're here—not there." Francesco waves to a man who's been a hired hand in the vegetable fields many times. The man stares, then smiles uncertainly and waves back. "All right." Francesco beckons us into a huddle. "I'm going off to talk. You do the same."

"How can I be friendly if I can't speak English?" mutters Giuseppe.

"You drank and ate with people when we lived in New Orleans, and you were no better at English then than you are now. What, Giuseppe? You want us to talk to no one but each other for the rest of our lives? They're the first ones who have treated us nice since we got here. If you don't understand, stuff your mouth with food and nod. Keep smiling and you'll have a good time." Francesco straightens up tall and marches off.

It's funny, because I think of Francesco as strong and blustery. But the way he squared his shoulders just now, I can tell he's trying to be brave.

We watch him disappear into the throng and I sense my uncles' spirits flag. They'll feel worse when I leave, too. Where is Patricia?

"Hi, stranger." A hand clamps down on my shoulder. It's Charles.

Rock is beside him. He clamps a hand on Cirone's shoulder. "Hey, Dancer."

Cirone smiles slow, almost shy. "Hi."

"Your foot all right?"

"Fine," says Cirone. "It was fine the next day."

"Ben said it: you got spirit, Dancer. He off playing the graduate, by the way," Charles says to me, as though I'd asked. "Y'all see the seat of his pants?"

"No," I say. I don't understand the question.

"Big and round. Someone put a throne back there." Charles laughs.

I look at Rock for an explanation.

"Ben shaking hands with everyone, like some king," says Rock.

Charles kicks the dirt. "The graduate. I be doing it in another couple of years."

"I'll shake King Ben's hand," I say.

"Shake it now," says Charles. "Come with us." He leads the way.

"No," I say.

"Huh?" Charles turns.

"I'm going to stay with my uncles awhile."

Rock glances over at Giuseppe and Carlo and Rosario. They're standing in a row with their hands folded in front of their bellies, looking vaguely stunned. Rock nods to me. "See y'all later."

"I'll come," says Cirone, not shy at all.

The three of them leave. Cirone abandoned me. But, hey, if I'd seen Patricia by now, I'd have left him behind, too.

Rosario sidles up to me. "Looking for someone?" He winks. "Patricia," he sings very very softly right into my ear. "Patricia, Patricia."

My cheeks go hot. Thank heavens the others can't hear. "She's just a friend."

"I've seen how you are with her," whispers Rosario. "I felt like that about a girl back in New Orleans." Before I can protest, he jerks his chin. "Look! Joe Evans. Come on."

"You don't speak English any better than us," says Giuseppe.

"Like Francesco says, we eat and smile. Come on."

"Not me," says Carlo.

Rosario leaves. Giuseppe rubs the back of his neck, then trails after him.

It's just Carlo and me.

"All that food," says Carlo. "I'm going to find new recipes. See you later."

Now I'm alone. Standing here like a dummy.

I follow Carlo. We sample pan-fried catfish, piles of mashed potatoes, green beans with cubes of lard floating in them, collards, black-eyed peas, steamed mustard greens. The whole time my eyes search.

There she is. Two tables up. Patricia digs a spoon into a pie. It's been so long, I feel I hardly remember her. She's beautiful. I move along, winding around people. But by the time I get there, she's disappeared.

So has Carlo.

Well, all right; I'm alone. Time to feast. I taste every meat—muskrat, swamp rabbit, chicken, loggerhead turtle. Is this the turtle that attacked Cirone's foot?

There's our 'gator. Everyone's saying it's tasty. The beast of that night is long gone. This is just meat. I take a nibble; it wakes my tongue. My tight neck and shoulders finally loosen. Now that I'm not so nervous, I realize I know lots of these people. Mostly the women. They're servants— I sell them vegetables.

And there's Patricia again. An old man pulls her into a hug, practically crushing her. Now the old woman beside him is kissing her.

I try to catch her eye.

Ah, the next table holds desserts. One is bread pudding, full of pecans, and oh, sweet Mother of God, that's it for me. Bread pudding, ah, bread pudding is heaven.

I eat slowly, trying not to feel lost. I see people laughing with my uncles. Just about every time I spy Patricia, she's laughing with someone, too. She's got the brightest teeth.

The church bell rings and Patricia's uncle Paul holds up a hand. He makes a speech about the graduates, who look proud. And the whole crowd says, "Amen."

A man leads us in prayer and everyone closes their eyes.

But I can't. Patricia looks soft and floaty in her pale yellow dress. Her hair hangs loose over her shoulders, glossy and thick, all wavy from being in braids most of the time. Her lips glisten.

Everyone sings "We'll walk in the light, the beautiful light." Then another song. And another. And another.

A band plays and people dance, singing along. Where's Patricia gone?

A man comes through the crowd announcing, "No spitting. No card playing. No crap shooting. No whisky drinking. No cursing. This here celebration is for the young-uns. Just dancing and singing."

Another man calls out dance figures and everyone's spinning each other, raising hands high for a clap.

"Give it a try," says a voice from behind. Rock. I think I like him best of the three boys. "Come on," says Rock. "It ain't hard to conquer. Just do what I do."

If I dance, I won't be able to keep my eye out for Patricia. "Later."

"Y'all better stir now, before the party over." Rock gives me a light punch in the arm. "I need to find Dancer and Charles. They ain't no scaredy-cats." He walks off.

And there's Patricia. I finally catch her eye. I lift a hand, but a girlfriend whisks her off to dance.

Before I know it, people are kissing goodbye. It's not that late; the party can't be over yet. No! Two girls pass me with their arms wrapped around each other's waists. That's how girls in Tallulah like to walk together. Bumping along, half tripping each other.

Francesco gathers us. "Time to leave."

"It can't be." My voice comes out as a whine. I want to snatch it back, but I can't help it. The bowl I made is still in the wagon. I couldn't give it to Patricia without breaking through a circle of friends—and that would have made it seem like some big thing, when all it is is a bowl.

"Get in the back," says Francesco.

I look around one last time. Patricia must have gone inside the church.

I lift the bowl from the wagon and race off.

"You be quick," Francesco calls after me.

I'm going into the back of the church when I almost smack into Patricia. "Here." I thrust the bowl into her hands. "Congratulations."

"Thank you." She lifts it up and down. "A bunch of ferns with a rock in the middle?"

"I made it for you." I'm walking backward down the path. "It's nothing."

"Thanks for nothing, then." She's walking toward me.

It takes me a second to get it. Then I laugh.

"Where you going?"

"Home."

"Stay while I open it, at least."

"Francesco's in the wagon. He said be quick."

"You always do things on time? Like a clock?"

"Don't you?"

"Sometimes the clock slow."

I smile.

"Sometimes it behind something, so you don't even see it."

I smile bigger.

"Sometimes ain't no clock at all."

I laugh. "But you don't know Francesco. If he says quick, he means it."

"Well, then, I'll wait to open this present till I see you again."

Good. That way I have to see her again soon. "Congratulations."

"Thank you. Y'all get enough to eat?"

"More than enough. Good night, Patricia."

"Night, Calogero. Sweet dreams." Her voice teases.

The wagon is already lurching through the grass. I have to run and catch the side boards and throw myself on.

Cirone grabs me by the seat of my pants and lugs me up. I scramble to the front of the wagon bed and sit with my arms hugging my knees.

I talked to her. I've talked to her so many times, but it was never like this. This time she couldn't think it was accidental, just me happening to be in her path. She knows I came to find her. I talked to her and she was funny. She's always funny.

"They ate them all." Carlo sits with his legs straight out in front of him and a pile of pie tins on his lap. "Every single one."

"Ten pies," I say.

"What do you mean, ten? Twelve. Americans do things by the dozen."

"Twelve." I give a whistle of approval. Americans do that, too.

"They loved them," says Carlo.

"What did you think of that alligator?" Rosario asks Carlo. In the moonlight I see him picking things out from between his teeth. And he's looking at me all sly. Why?

"Pepper," says Carlo, and he shakes his head. "Too much." He rubs his hands together. "One of the graduates prepared it. A girl."

A girl? I look at Cirone.

"Patricia," Cirone whispers in my ear.

"How do you know?"

"Charles told everyone."

I remember when Charles caught that alligator. He said Patricia was going to make a special portion for me.

And she asked me if I'd had enough to eat.

And I said, "More than enough." Oh, no. That could mean I didn't like it. I finally get up the nerve to talk to her and that's what I say.

What must she think?

fourteen

We get home and take care of the wagon and horse, and Cirone and I go to bed while the men sit on the porch. They sit right on the floor—that's our new tradition. After all, it's a wood floor now, as Francesco likes to point out, just like Dr. Hodge's. They smoke cigars and drink *limoncello* and talk softly. The goats tramp around them and make their *nee-haw* noises.

I lie in bed fully dressed with a sheet pulled up to my neck and wait and wait. The night cools down a bit, but I'm drenched in sweat, practically ready to jump out of my skin by the time the men finally haul off to bed.

When the room is a chorus of snores, I get up and pad softly through the kitchen. Dried butter beans and okra and garlic hang from the ceiling. I work my way around them to the porch, tie my shoes on, and run.

This is crazy. If Francesco finds out, I'm a dead man.

But even without Francesco, this is crazy. I know where Patricia lives. That day I walked her home we could see her house at the end of the path when Charles and Ben and Rock stopped us. It looks like every two-room tenant-farmer shack. How on earth will I get her to come outside without waking up everyone else?

No answer comes. But I'm still running.

More than enough.

I want to kick myself for saying that.

The quickest way is to pass through town and out the other side. I take Walnut Street at a run. Families are walking home from the ice cream saloon down the center of the road. Sidewalks line the major streets of Tallulah, but no one uses them at night. So I can run free there.

A little girl rides on her daddy's shoulders. I carried Rocco like that sometimes. He laughed when I'd prance and make him bounce. I've got to get him over here soon.

The little girl points at me. "That your goat?"

I stop and turn around. Bedda trots up and bangs her head into my legs.

"Go home, Bedda," I mutter in Sicilian.

The little girl laughs, and her family hurries on by.

I should have used English in front of them. But Bedda doesn't understand English. At least, that's what Francesco says.

Bedda rams me again. I look around. She's alone. It's odd for a goat to go trotting off alone. She should want to go back to the others.

"Get out of here, Bedda."

She jumps up and puts her front hooves on my chest, like a dog. I'm not going to run all the way back home to tie her up. She'd only kick at whatever I tied her to and then Francesco would wake and everything would be ruined. Dr. Hodge is right: goats should be penned up at night. Francesco is a maniac to say goats need their freedom. And Carlo is a fool to back him up and say cheese from free goats tastes better. The truth is, Francesco loves these stupid goats, especially Bedda.

I'll just have to lose her. I run through the streets this way and that. Bedda stays at my heels. I hide behind trees, but she finds me. I shout at her, but she only rams me.

Then I get an idea. I know it's terrible of me, but what can I do? I run past Dr. Hodge's house. And just like that Bedda leaves me and trots up onto Dr. Hodge's porch. Why, I don't know. But in this moment I'm just grateful.

I run flat out. The night is full of croaks from the little ponds all around. Insects fly into my face with a small *crack*. It's still warm. Running through this heavy, humid air feels almost like swimming. But I don't slow down.

Finally, I'm in front of Patricia's place. I lean forward and push my hands against my knees to rest as I catch my breath. Not a single lamp shines in that house. If I peek in a window, I'm liable to get a smack on the head. Or worse.

I walk slowly around the house. Something screeches and runs across my path. I stop short. Just a cat. A dog would rip me apart, me sneaking around like this. Something sits on the ground outside one window. A pile of crumpled ferns. Like the ones I wrapped the bowl in. Patricia stood inside that window, for sure.

What's the worst that could happen? Her uncles might yell at me. They're not going to have a loaded shotgun waiting by the window.

Are they?

I crouch down under the window and whisper loudly, "Patricia."

I wait forever.

This is insane. If anyone heard me, they're going to bonk me over the head with a plank of wood. I straighten up and walk back toward the path.

"Y'all sure give up easy." Patricia's standing out front in that soft yellow dress. She walks up to me.

I want to touch her arm. "I liked the 'gator."

"Come all this way just to tell me that?" The tips of her teeth shine white in the moonlight.

"No. I loved the 'gator. It was the best thing I've ever eaten."

"The best, huh?"

"The very best."

"Well, if that's all you got to say, then good night." She turns to go.

"Wait."

She spins on her heel.

"I didn't know you had a cat." How dumb can I get?

"I didn't know you was a artist."

"You opened my present. I saw the ferns on the ground outside the window. You said you wouldn't open it till you saw me again."

"I saw you," says Patricia. "I saw you in my head."

I don't know what to say to that.

"I like the bowl," she says.

"Really?"

"No. I love it." She giggles.

"Want to take a walk?"

"Sure."

"Don't you want to put shoes on first?"

"What for? Shoes make feet tender. I got strong feet and I aim to keep them strong."

"You had shoes on at the party."

"I got a mother, too."

I laugh. "You make everything so . . . simple . . . I mean . . ."

"Y'all calling me simple?" But she's laughing, too.

Flustered, I turn and walk off the path.

"Not that way," Patricia whispers loud. "That way the outhouse."

"Oh."

"It be moving all the time."

"What?"

"In the wintertime it's too far away; in the summer too close."

It takes me a minute to catch her joke. I laugh. "I was in your classroom. I held a book."

"Y'all ain't never held a book before?"

"Of course I did." But I didn't hold a book you'd held. "I went to school in Sicily. Until my mother died."

"I didn't know." Patricia's voice goes soft. "Sorry you lost your mamma." She walks ahead now, then turns to face me, so she's walking backward and I'm walking forward. It's just like we were at the church earlier tonight, only I was the one walking backward then. "Ever hear they's seventeen thousand Eye-talians in Louisiana?"

I shake my head. "How do you know?"

"The United States Census of 1890 told me." She turns and skips a few steps, then turns back to face me again. "Well, not actually them. Miss Clarrie. My teacher. During sugar-cane season they's more, because Eye-talians come from all over to work the harvest." She points at me and smiles. "Most of them Sicilian. Like y'all. That's what my teacher say."

"Your teacher is smart."

"The smartest woman in the world. Ugly, too. Ugly as a mud fence in a rainstorm."

"A mud fence?"

"It just mean she really ugly. But that's good."

"Good? How come?"

"A pretty woman get married. And a married woman ain't allowed to teach."

"What do you like best about her? I mean, besides that she's the smartest woman in the world."

"She taught us to ask. Never be afeared to look dumb. 'Cause looking dumb don't matter. Being dumb, that matter. So just ask. And if you don't get a straight answer, then go seeking. No matter what it is. Just go seeking."

I'm suddenly ashamed. I should ask, then. "What's the United States Census?"

Patricia laughs. "Every ten years our government send people door-to-door collecting information. Who live here? What color? What religion? You know."

"Why do they want to know that?"

"I'm not sure. But I'm glad."

"Because then you know how many Eye-talians there are in Louisiana?" I say, joking.

"That, and 'cause when the census takers went around after the big war, they found slaves who didn't know they wasn't slaves no more."

Prickles run up my arms. "How could people not know?"

"My grandmother didn't. My mother was seven years old in 1870 when a census taker came to the door and told her they was free. Five years after the war ended."

139

Slaves five years longer than they had to be. I feel like some giant animal has stomped on me.

A hoot comes from far off, then a screech.

"Know what that was?" asks Patricia.

"No."

"A barred owl just caught him a snake. I hope it was a coral snake. They look so pretty and act so mean. Why, a coral snake would do his grandma out of her supper if he had a chance." She turns and skips ahead again. Skips barefoot, after talking about a coral snake.

I run and catch up.

A *rat-a-tat* comes from somewhere ahead.

"Ivory-billed woodpecker," says Patricia. "See that bit of white?" She points.

"I don't see a thing."

"It's hard in the dark. He big and fat—the biggest woodpecker of all. But he black, so the night hide him, even his red crest. All you can see is that bright white bill. Look up in that old tree. They like the oldest trees. There. See him?"

And I do now. A little speck of white.

"Looking for a mate," says Patricia.

"Is that what his pecking means?"

"When the beats come regular. If they come all crazy, then you just got one hungry bird, pecking for grubs."

"And that?" I point where something flew low. "What was that?"

"Hush." Patricia puts her hand on my arm to still me.

Her hand is warm and soft.

After a while the call sings out.

"I thought so. A nightjar."

"It flew like the bats in Sicily."

"Both of them swoop low to catch insects."

"You said you know everything about birds. It's true. How'd you learn?"

She takes her hand off my arm.

In a flash of courage, I catch that hand.

She doesn't pull away.

We're hand in hand. It doesn't matter where we go now, we're hand in hand.

"Uncle Bill used to take all us young-uns out for hikes. Day and night. The others didn't care. But I learned. And it mattered."

"How?"

"I got sick when I was eight. Ran a fever all winter. Couldn't eat, could barely drink. I had to stop school. For the whole year after that, Mamma was too afeared to let me go to school. She thought I might catch something even worse and die. All I did was stay by the window and listen to the birds."

"That must have been hard, being sick."

"Sure. But it was wonderful learning birds right. I love their calls. They use music to talk. And they chatterboxes like you wouldn't believe. They talk all the time. Less at night, but if you pay attention, you hear them. Listen."

I listen. At first there's nothing. Then . . . "You're right. The night's full of birdcalls."

"Not them frogs. Listen to the other ones. The far-off calls."

I strain. And there they are. Distant and soft with long silence between.

"Whip-poor-wills," she says. "Anyway, I missed two years of school. I had to study extra hard to graduate lower school on time."

"I knew you were smart."

She stops in her tracks. "You trying to butter me up for a kiss?"

I feel all crazy. I've never kissed a girl. I step toward her.

She points past me. I look. "The edge of town. You know what they do to you if they see you kiss a colored girl?"

I step closer. "I don't care."

"You got no idea."

I kiss her. And she kisses me back. Warm and sweet and wet.

"Good night, Calogero," she says right into my mouth. "You got soft lips. They feel nice." She steps away.

All I want is to pull her to me again. But I don't. "I'll walk you back home."

"No you won't. You too slow. I'm running."

I hold her hand tighter. "Don't run. Cirone and I saw a panther. They chase runners."

"Silly. Ain't enough trees between here and home for a panther to feel safe. I'm running."

"What's the hurry?"

"Every human being got his race to run."

"Is that a riddle or something?"

She smiles. "My mamma say that. I got mine. You got yours. Be quick!" And she's gone, yellow folding into the black air in the time it takes to stop feeling her hand in mine.

I walk along Depot Street, going pole to pole, touching them—for no other reason than that they're there. They go all the way to New Orleans in one direction and New York in the other, and to farther places, to the whole rest of the world. The wires linking those poles carry telegraph messages. And those new things—telephone messages. Frank Raymond told me half a dozen people in town already have those gadgets.

The street is deserted. Every store has closed for the night. It's peaceful. Wonderful. I run in a long lope. I'm not in any hurry, it just feels good. The sky is star-spangled from horizon to horizon. I turn up a side street.

"Damn goats!" Dr. Hodge has a broom in his hands, swiping at the rear of two goats.

I race to the next corner. But not fast enough. Bedda heads straight for me. And Bruttu, the billy, is right behind her. He must have come looking for her.

"Are those your goats?" shouts Dr. Hodge. "You one of those damned dagoes?"

He can't possibly recognize me in the dark. But my heart bangs.

"Next time I'll shoot them. I'll shoot them dead. And you, too."

I run as if the devil's chasing.

fifteen

Sunday afternoon I'm walking home from Frank Raymond's. I told him today that I'm going to Patricia's school in autumn, so I wanted painting lessons instead of tutoring from now on. But he told me he's leaving town at the end of the month anyway. He likes to wander—see the world. The thought of him disappearing makes me feel strange. I still can't believe it.

At least there are four more Sundays left in this month, so we can paint till he goes. Today was a good lesson. I made a birthday present for Rocco—a picture of an owl.

The paint is drying. I'll go back for it before supper tomorrow. Rocco will like it. The owl's eyes glitter.

I turn the corner. Three boys stand over a boy on his side. One of them is kicking him! The boy is curled around his middle, his hands over his cap, groaning. It's Cirone!

"Stop!" I run up and grab the kicker by the elbow.

He stumbles aside in surprise, but in the same moment I'm shoved hard from behind. My chin smacks on the sidewalk and I hear a crack inside my head. I roll onto my back, cradling my chin.

"Watch where you going. You bumped me," says one of the boys.

"Yeah, y'all blind or something? The both of you dagoes, blind as bats."

"Stupid is more like it."

"Are you stupid, boy?"

"All dagoes is stupid."

Three pink faces glare down at me.

I look past their legs. Cirone's still on his side, silent now, but he's rocking his head, so I know he's conscious.

My chin bleeds into my palm. I lean to the side and spit out half a tooth.

"Ha! How many teeth you planning on losing today? That's only number one."

None of this makes sense. I don't recognize any of these boys. What was Cirone doing here? Did he do something to them?

I look around. A man turns up the sidewalk, sees us, and crosses to the other side. There's no one else about. Maybe they all ducked inside when they saw what was up.

I keep one hand on my chin and pick up my cap with the other.

A boy kicks the cap out of my hand, giving my fingers a wicked blow.

I don't move.

This must be how Joseph felt when he was still Uruna, when the boys buried him alive. He must have known where it was going.

Cirone must have known, too. Does he realize I'm here now? Please, Lord, tell him he's not alone.

I keep looking at them.

"Playing dumb?"

"Y'all speak English. Don't pretend you don't."

"Yeah, talk."

"Who cares if you talk, anyhow? We saw you. And we told. Oh, yeah, we told on you good. The whole town's talking now."

"And y'all know what they's talking about?"

Patricia. They must have seen me kiss Patricia last night. She said I didn't know what they'd do if they saw. Cirone got beat up for something I did.

I pull my elbows in close, ready to punch. Giuseppe taught me how to fight when I arrived—said it would come in handy. I thought it was just Giuseppe being grumpy. I look over at Cirone. Oh, yeah, they're going to beat me up, but I'm going to make it hard for them.

"They's talking about how y'all went to a darkie gathering. All you dagoes."

"Eating the same food, from the same plates."

"Disgusting."

"I saw you licking each other's fingers."

"Really? Ain't that something. I'd have vomited if I saw that."

My breath comes free again. They don't know about Patricia. They won't do anything to her. "We were at school," I say. "Sicilians are allowed at that school."

"Ain't no school in summer. That was a party."

"Fraternizing with them cotton pickers. That's what Pa calls it. Fraternizing."

"Next thing you know, y'all be giving the darkies ideas."

"Fraternizing and big ideas. And selling stuff too cheap."

"Yeah. Making deals with the dagoes in New Orleans."

"Ruining the company stores."

"What you doing?" A woman stands in the street. Mrs. Rogers' Lila.

"Mind your own business."

I hate him sneering at her like that, but that's good advice. These boys aren't likely to care what Lila thinks, not with the color of her skin.

"I work for Mrs. Rogers." Lila comes up onto the

sidewalk. She looks over at Cirone, who's managed to work himself to a sit by now. He's hugging his knees and still rocking his head. "These boys the greengrocers Mrs. Rogers buy from. Mrs. Rogers' favorite grocer boys."

"Mr. Rogers don't like dagoes," says one boy. "I heard him say that."

"And Willy Rogers, he hates them," says another. "He says we ought to run them out of town. Ain't a single one worth spitting at."

"Mr. Rogers like to eat," says Lila. "Willy do, too. These their favorite grocer boys. Stand back."

The boys don't move.

Lila steps forward with a loud noise through her nose. Almost a bugle sound.

One boy takes a step away. The other two follow suit.

"Get up, child," she says to me.

I get to my feet and help Cirone up. He stays bent, both hands on his belly.

"See you in the morning. At the stand." She looks at the boys. "Like always."

My cap lies behind one of the boys. I know I'm pushing my luck, but I already lost a hat on the 'gator hunt. I don't want to know what Francesco will do if I lose this cap. Besides, pride gets the best of me. I walk past that boy. Our chests are only a foot apart. He tenses up. I reach behind him and grab my cap. I put it on and touch the tip of it in farewell to Lila.

Cirone and I walk away. Slowly.

It takes a long time for my thoughts to unscramble.

"How bad does it hurt?"

Cirone straightens a little. "No blood." He looks at me. "Your chin's a mess."

"What were you doing in town?"

He turns his head away and straightens a little more.

"Come on, tell me."

"Where did you go last night, huh?" Cirone presses on his belly with both hands and takes a deep breath. "You're not the only one with secrets." He puts a fist to his mouth and chews on a knuckle. "Calo, don't tell what they said about fraternizing. You do, and that's the end of parties. That's the end of everything good here."

I lick blood off my bottom lip. "I want us to go to every party we get invited to."

"Right. It makes me mad when they say we can't be friends with Negroes. They don't want us with whites and they don't want us with Negroes. They think Sicilians belong nowhere, with no one. Like we're not people at all."

"Well, we are."

We hook arms and cross the grass.

sixteen

"Rotten kids." Carlo picks dirt and tiny pebbles from my chin. He heated water to wash the gash. This last picking part hurts like mad. He makes hissing noises as he works. He knows he's hurting me and I think it bothers him more than me. "Nasty little no-goods," mutters Carlo. And he doesn't even know about my broken tooth.

Or about Cirone's bruises. They're hidden under his clothes. But my chin was out in the open.

Francesco comes through the door and takes me in with one swift glance. He glowers. "What did you do now?"

"Me? It's not my fault. They jumped me."

"Who?" snaps Giuseppe. He followed Francesco in, with Rosario at his heels.

"Three boys."

Rosario looks quick at Cirone. "What about you?"

"I was out back. Nowhere near."

Cirone lies good. How much practice has he had?

Francesco looks over Carlo's shoulder to inspect my wounds. "How old? What did they say?"

"My age, maybe. They said all dagoes are stupid."

"Oh yeah? Did they say what we do that makes us so stupid?"

"Something about deals with dagoes in New Orleans."

Francesco gives a *harumph.* "Is that everything?"

I'm working on keeping my eyes steady.

"Come on, Calo. What else did they say?"

"That we're ruining the company stores," I mumble.

"Enough!" growls Giuseppe. "They've got to be stopped."

"Sit!" Francesco points to the benches. "Everyone but Carlo and Calogero."

Giuseppe shakes his head, but he drops onto a bench. The others do, too.

Francesco crosses his arms on the table and leans onto them. "We have to talk this over. Make sure we do the right thing."

"We do nothing," says Rosario. "They're just kids."

I'm with Rosario; this has to end here. If Giuseppe

makes a fuss with those boys, they'll torment Cirone and me every time they catch one of us alone.

"Kids." Giuseppe shakes his head. "Kids don't talk about business. This is coming from their fathers. We all know the price of cotton keeps dropping. They're hurting, and they need their company stores to make a profit. But everyone's buying from us instead. This is a warning. And if we let it go, if we don't stop them cold, it'll be New Orleans all over again."

Everyone hushes.

My skin tightens. "What are you talking about?"

Carlo holds me by the ear. "Don't move your jaw while I'm cleaning your chin."

I put up my hand to block Carlo's wash cloth. "Tell me," I say to Giuseppe. "What happened in New Orleans?"

Rosario looks sideways at Cirone. "It's not worth talking about."

"Is it about lynching?"

The men gape at me. Cirone's face changes. He looks as if he might vomit.

"So you know about it?" asks Francesco.

"No. Tell us. Tell Cirone and me."

"They need to know," says Giuseppe to Rosario. His voice sounds sadder than I've ever heard it. "It's starting all over again. They need to know."

"Don't be absurd," says Rosario. "In New Orleans it started because of a gun. We don't carry guns."

I look at Francesco. He carried a shotgun that day he was mad at Willy Rogers. But he doesn't speak up, and neither does Carlo. The others saw that gun in the corner before Francesco put it away—but they don't know the story behind it. It's our secret. That's so odd. Probably everyone else in Tallulah knows why Francesco had a shotgun that day, but Rosario and Giuseppe and Cirone don't—and no one's going to tell them.

"They should know," says Francesco at last. "They're Sicilian."

"No," says Rosario. "Cirone was only five when it happened. He had nightmares. He didn't stop till we moved up here. It's behind us now. He's forgotten."

"Right," says Carlo. He comes over, put both hands on the table, and slowly lowers himself to the bench as though he's become ancient in a second. "We got away from all that. It doesn't help anyone to bring it up again."

I look at Cirone sitting on the bench near Rosario. "Do you want to know about New Orleans, Cirone?"

His eyes lock on mine. "Yes."

"Tell us," I say to Francesco.

"They lynched eleven men," says Francesco.

"Hold it," says Giuseppe. "Let me tell it. From the beginning. Rosario and I were there. You and Carlo weren't."

"I thought you all came over together," I say.

"Carlo and I followed," says Francesco. "We were supposed to come a couple of months later—but then there was all that trouble and we waited to see what would happen. We waited so long, it was the next summer before we got on a ship."

Giuseppe points to the spot on the bench beside Cirone. "Sit down, Calogero."

This is going to be awful. Numbness creeps up the sides of my head, making my ears ring. I sit on the edge of the bench.

"These are the facts," says Giuseppe. "First, just the facts. Six days after Rosario and Cirone and I got off the boat, on the night of the fifteenth of October, 1890, David Hennessy, the big chief—"

"The police commissioner," says Francesco.

"The police commissioner of New Orleans, he got shot," says Giuseppe. "He died the next morning. But before he died, he said, 'Dagoes did it.' "

"Dagoes." Carlo shakes his head. "You'd think he was some ignorant, backward man to say such a word— as ignorant as those rotten boys. But he was the police commissioner."

"Who are you kidding?" says Francesco. "Some of the richest men in America call us dagoes. Not to mention that piece of garbage, Willy Rogers. I should have taught him a lesson last month. Only I held back out of respect for Dr. Hodge's wishes."

I think of Dr. Hodge Saturday night, calling out as he chased the goats, asking if I was one of those damned dagoes. I hug myself to keep the shaking inside from showing.

"Let me finish," says Giuseppe. "Police came through our neighborhood with guns. We stayed inside, but, even so, they arrested over two hundred and fifty. Young, old, boys smaller than you two. They beat them. Then a committee indicted nineteen." He looks at the ceiling. "Nineteen for one murder." Giuseppe falls silent.

No one talks.

The silence goes on so long, my throat grows scratchy and I cough.

Giuseppe talks again: "They decided to have two trials, the first for nine men—the second for the rest.

"The first started the last day of February 1891. The press said Italians were murderers; all of us, Mafia. Suddenly people threw that word at us anywhere we went. In their eyes we were all criminal.

"Still, the jury listened fairly. Six men were found not guilty. For the other three the jury was undecided. There was no translator, and those men spoke so little English, they couldn't answer questions. It was a mistrial. This was announced March thirteenth. They put all nine men in the prison overnight." Giuseppe stops and clears his throat.

"The next day the newspaper called for a mass meeting at Canal and Royal streets. Thousands came. More joined as they marched through town. By the time they reached Congo Square, they say there were twenty thousand.

Twenty thousand stormed the prison." Giuseppe's voice becomes monotonous. He talks as though he's said these words in his head a thousand times before.

"The warden, he was honest, like the jurors. He wouldn't turn the prisoners over. So the mob went around back and beat down the gate.

"The warden locked all the prisoners in their cells except the Sicilians. He told the Sicilians to scatter—hide in the women's section—do anything to save themselves.

"The mob shot nine inside the prison. So many bullets . . . their bodies were destroyed. Another one, Emmanuele, they found him muttering in his cell. Everyone knew he was crazy. They hanged him from a streetlamp, and when he tried to climb the rope, they shot him. Twenty-eight years old and . . . demented, and . . . they still shot him." Giuseppe pauses and I see his chest shudder. "The last one they found . . . he was pretending to be dead. They hanged him from a tree. Shot him, too.

"Eleven men. Murdered.

"Society ladies came out to see. Dipped handkerchiefs in the blood. Souvenirs." Giuseppe stops. He's crying.

Rosario puts his hand on Cirone's shoulder. Cirone keeps staring at Giuseppe.

I lay my hands on the table. "Didn't anybody do anything to the lynchers?"

"Italy threatened war," says Giuseppe. "Louisiana argued that the men were Americans. But only two had become

American citizens. The rest were Italians. Italy was enraged. And that is why I will never give up my Italian citizenship. Never."

"But there was no war, right?" I say. I was only six back in 1891, but I would have heard if there was a war.

"Italy settled," says Rosario, bitter.

"A grand jury looked into the lynchings," says Giuseppe. "Two months later they said the mob was responsible citizens protecting the public from danger." He puts his hands on his forehead in a gesture of agony. "We should have been the responsible citizens. Not them."

"What? What do you mean?" It's so hard to see Giuseppe like this.

"We Sicilians. We should have armed ourselves and defended the prison. Instead, we hid. I hid." Giuseppe buries his face in his hands. "For days."

"I did, too," says Rosario. "We had to."

"You had Cirone to look after. I hid like a rat."

"No one could do anything," says Rosario. "They would have killed us. You know that. You sat beside me and listened as people read us the newspapers. You heard how that animal Theodore Roosevelt called the lynchings 'a rather good thing.' And that congressman from Massachusetts, that Henry Cabot Lodge, he said we were filth. All of America was against us." Revulsion spreads across Rosario's face. "Still, Italy settled."

"What could Italy do?" says Carlo. "President Harrison

said he deplored the lynchings. He gave money to the dead men's families. Italy had to agree. Besides, war is no answer."

Everyone's out of words. Giuseppe's hands still cover his face.

"Now the rest," I say. "Giuseppe?"

"What?" Giuseppe opens his hands and looks at me with a tired face.

"You said the facts first. What's the rest? Who killed the police commissioner?"

Giuseppe gives a sad little laugh. "I don't know. It never really mattered. No one talked about him anymore. Once the lynching had been declared reasonable, people started complaining about the Italians. Posters went up. People said Italians monopolized the produce business. And fishing. They said we had taken all the jobs for peddlers and tinkers and cobblers."

"So everyone fired us," says Rosario. "Overnight, we were all out of work."

"The only place that would hire us was the plantations," says Giuseppe. "That was the point of the lynchings in the first place."

"What?"

"I'll tell this part," says Francesco. "I know this part as well as anyone." He studies his hands. "After the Civil War so many Negroes went North, the plantation owners didn't have enough people to do the labor the slaves used to do. So they brought in Chinese. But the Chinese wouldn't put up with the bad conditions and the lousy pay. So the plantation owners brought in Sicilians."

"They put up posters in Palermo," says Rosario. "They said everything would be terrific. We fell for it. Who could help it? We were desperate in Italy. Dirt poor."

"We came," says Francesco, "so many Sicilian men, and we worked their plantations. They made fun of how we eat and talk. And all we did in return was work. Sugarcane work is backbreaking. You swing heavy machetes in the scorching heat while the mosquitoes eat you alive. In autumn you work overtime at night in the sugar mills, grinding, boiling, refining. We got skinny as rails. Worked hard as dogs. Dogs! Because to us thirty or forty dollars for a harvest season of sugarcane was a fortune."

"So why do they hate us?" I ask.

"Simple," says Giuseppe. "We're not dogs." The look of raw pain on his face scares me. "We're smart. We made gardens on slopes no one wanted and sold vegetables. We caught fish and oysters in the Gulf. We fed ourselves easy. We made friends of the South Americans, and traded with their fruit boats. We were good at Spanish. We had our own businesses fast. We didn't have to work on their stinking plantations anymore."

"That's why they lynched those men," says Francesco. "Hennessy's murder was just an excuse to put Sicilians back on the plantations. That's why they keep bringing over more of us. They're so convinced we're dumb animals, they can't believe we're good at business—they see it, and they still don't believe. The lynchings were supposed to teach us a lesson, put us in our place."

"But we showed them," says Rosario. "Today Sicilians run the dock-import business again. Like before."

"New Orleans is a good place to live now," says Francesco. "But we didn't know it would turn around. So as soon as we had enough to buy land, we came up here."

"To someplace without Sicilians," says Rosario. "Someplace where no one already hated us."

"Beppe came over with Salvatore months later," says Carlo. "But they went to Milliken's Bend so that it wouldn't seem like too many of us in one place. The plantation owners get afraid when there's too many."

"A fresh start," says Francesco.

"Ha!" says Giuseppe. "We didn't understand." He's silent. Then, "We're hated everywhere."

I remember Cirone saying everyone hates us, the night we met the boys picking up manure on Depot Street. I shake my head. "That can't be."

"Carlo?" Giuseppe jerks his chin at Carlo. "Get the newspapers."

Carlo goes to a chest. He digs down to the bottom, and comes out with an armload of newspapers wrapped in blue paper. He sets them on the table.

"Read, Calogero," says Giuseppe. "You know how. Read to Cirone. Our friends in New Orleans pack newspapers in the fruit crates. Every time someone writes something bad about Italians, they send it. We can't read them, but we know what they say because it's always the same. Why should Tallulah be different?"

"Tallulah is different!" The blood pounds my head. "My friends don't hate us."

"Sit down, Calogero," says Francesco.

I hadn't even realized I'd stood up. I sit again.

"You're right," says Francesco. "They're good people."

"It's never been the Negroes who hate us," says Rosario.

"Never?" Cirone leans forward. It's the first word he's said so far.

Rosario nods. "We got on fine with them in New Orleans."

"But that made the whites hate us more," says Giuseppe. "They were afraid the Negroes would get fed up with the terrible conditions on the plantations and strike or quit, because that's what Sicilians do. They passed laws against commingling—that's what they called it. They frightened the Negroes from being our friends."

"But it's different here," says Francesco.

I look at Cirone. Fraternizing with the Negroes. That's what the boys said; that's why they came after us. Cirone's face is blank as he looks back at me.

"Calo's chin," says Giuseppe. "What are we going to do about that?"

"This will cool down," says Carlo. "We don't want

trouble. That just plays into their hands. That just convinces them they're right about us."

"I agree," says Rosario.

Francesco sighs. "I don't know."

Giuseppe doesn't speak.

"We're in the middle of a good season," says Carlo, his voice very soft. "Independence Day is in just two days. Business, Francesco."

Francesco nods. "And then there's the big ball next week."

"Right," says Carlo. "Right. The town needs us. We can make a lot of money. We're just six little people—six. They can't really see us as a threat. This will pass. If we let it. We're strong inside." He's almost whispering now. "We can let this pass."

Francesco's eyes wander.

"Like you said." Rosario turns to Francesco, speaking as quietly as Carlo did. "We've got friends now. Imagine the good times ahead."

Francesco slaps a hand on the table. I flinch at the sudden loudness. "We're businessmen. There's money to be made. We can't overreact." He points at me. "And you, Calogero, keep your eyes open. Don't let those boys catch you again." He looks at Giuseppe. "You hear me? This is how we'll do it. Don't make trouble."

"I won't," says Giuseppe. "But if it comes, I won't hide. Never again. I can't."

Francesco nods. "Fair enough."

We eat. Then I spend the evening reading to Cirone by the waning summer light. The newspapers say we're uncivilized, we're like animals. We carry stiletto knives and use them on anyone. I want to rip these pages to shreds. Why does Carlo save them?

Then I read about Dago Joe. Two years ago he was on his way to Shelby Depot to stand trial for the murder of a railroad agent in Memphis when a crowd hanged him. There was no evidence against him other than his low birth—that's what the newspaper said: "low." His father was Sicilian. Like me. His mother was Negro. Like Patricia.

I fold the newspapers back into the blue paper and set them on top of Carlo's trunk. Cirone and I wash our feet and get into bed. "Cirone," I whisper. "You going to start having nightmares again?"

"I never stopped," he whispers back.

seventeen

Granni and Docili are harnessed side by side to the front of the wagon. Giuseppe's on the driver's bench.

"Get in." Francesco jerks his chin toward the wagon bed. "Today is the best selling day for watermelons all season. Go up and down every town road."

"I've got to go to the post office." I picked up the owl painting from Frank Raymond this morning. He packaged it for me. "I have to mail a present to Rocco. For his birthday."

"You'll have plenty of time to go to the post office after you sell all the melons."

"All?" The wagon is big. "What if people don't want watermelons?"

"Tomorrow is the Fourth of July. They want watermelons."

Cirone and I climb into the back of the wagon.

"And, Calogero, when you pass men, remind them I'll have homemade *limoncello* in pint jars at the grocery today."

"Homemade *limoncello*. I'll remind them."

"And don't say anything about alcohol directly to the ladies, but you two can talk between you in front of ladies about the *limoncello*. To remind them, too."

We drive out to the field where Joe Evans is working. Patricia's uncles, Bill and Paul, are there, too. Francesco said he's going to use them regular on the fields now. I smile at them, hesitant at first. But they smile back big.

The three of them have already picked the melons and stacked them into a giant pile. It takes us more than half an hour to load the wagon, there are so many. I count as we go, but I lose track. Over two hundred. We'll make a fortune.

Cirone and I climb onto the driver's bench on either side of Giuseppe. We start at the northeast corner of town, stopping on every block and selling to every household. Francesco is right: the whole town wants melons. The trouble is, there aren't two hundred families in Tallulah. So how are we going to sell them all? I shout at the top of my lungs: "Watermelons! Big, ripe, juicy melons!"

The sun beats. I'm sweating so hard, when I carry a

166

melon to a doorstep, I have to hug it to my chest or it'll slip through my wet hands. We reach the western edge of town, go south a block, then head back across town on East Askew.

"Hey," calls a boy. He's with two others, smaller than him. They've been following us for the past block.

"Want a melon?" asks Cirone.

"How much?"

"Fifteen cents."

"Ain't got fifteen cents," says the boy.

Cirone looks at me. I nod. "How much you got?"

"Ain't got no money."

"Aw, get out of here," says Cirone. "Go away."

We sell melons to that block and move on to the next. The boys follow.

There are houses on both sides of the street now, so both Cirone and I have to deliver them. It's slow going. I hand a melon to a woman and take her fifteen cents when "Bang!" I run back to the wagon.

"Bang, bang, bang!" It's Giuseppe, shooting his finger like a gun at the back of the boys. They're running like mad, but they've got one of the biggest watermelons, and they're so little, they have to hold it among them, all three together. I'd laugh, except Giuseppe is shouting now in Sicilian, saying things about where thieves come from and where they ought to go. "Bang!" he shouts, his eyes popping.

And the littlest kid stumbles. The watermelon goes flying. *Smash*. There's red juicy melon all over the dusty road.

"Serves them right," says Giuseppe in Sicilian.

We finish this whole street, turn south, and then go west onto East Green Street. Some houses buy two melons. We've sold enough that there's room for Cirone and me in the back of the wagon now. If the sun wasn't so hot, everything would be good.

When we get to the western edge of town again, a girl hails us. Tall, with ropy arms, she squints through the sun at us. She holds a big osnaburg bag, long and white, the kind cotton pickers use. She comes up to the back of the wagon. "Who's boss?"

"Me," I say. After all, Giuseppe can't say more than a word or two.

"My brother, he got something to say."

I look past her. There's no one there. "Where's your brother?"

"Hiding behind them bushes."

I look at her and wait. "Is he going to come out?"

"Not if you yell."

I wipe the sweat off my forehead. "I won't yell."

"Come on out, Jerome."

The watermelon thief comes out from behind the bush. "You going to shoot me?"

"You know a finger's different from a gun, don't you?" I shake my head. "Nobody's going to shoot you."

"Bang!" shouts Giuseppe. He cocks his finger at the thief. "Bang, bang!"

The boy runs behind the bush. "Sorry," he shouts.

"Stop with the banging now, Giuseppe," I say in Sicilian. Then I turn to the girl. "Well, I guess that's done, then."

"No, it isn't," says Giuseppe in Sicilian. "He cost us a melon."

"Ain't settled yet." The sister lifts the bag. "Sweet potatoes. For that melon."

"We've got white potatoes in our own field," says Giuseppe in Sicilian. "They're better than those orange things."

"You keep them," I say.

"I can't abide a thief. We got to pay you."

I take the bag. "Thanks."

The girl doesn't go away.

"Well?"

"I need the bag back."

People save paper bags—they're expensive. But osnaburg bags are different. And this one is old and beat up. She must work the cotton fields. Maybe her boss makes her pay for a new one. I dump the sweet potatoes in among the watermelons and go to fold the sack when I think better of it and put a watermelon inside it instead. I hand it to her. "That was enough potatoes to pay for two melons."

"Don't do that," she says. "Jerome need to learn thieving ain't right."

"Maybe enough for three melons. But I docked you one, for the thieving."

She takes the sack and looks at me. "Put them potatoes in the fire when you roast your rabbit, or whatever you got, then when it turn to ashes, they be sweet as candy."

"I'll do that. You want me to carry this melon to your door?"

"We live outside town. I'll manage fine. Much obliged." She turns and goes.

"We got a melon?" Jerome the Thief sticks his head out from behind the bush. "We really got a melon?"

"Get on home," says the girl. She lugs that melon, following Jerome, who's laughing and singing, "Melon, melon, we got a melon."

"You've got no stomach for business," says Giuseppe in Sicilian.

"I saw that," comes a voice in English.

I turn around. "Good day, Mr. Johnson, sir."

Fred Johnson runs the general-goods store. He must be walking to work after dinner break. He takes a round tin out of his pocket and stuffs tobacco in his cheek. He points in the wagon. "How many sweet potatoes for that melon?" His tone is sarcastic.

"We're taking coins, sir," I say.

"Real business, huh? I just saw otherwise. I just saw an ar-range-ment." He draws out the word. "That's what you do with them darkie cotton pickers. Ar-range-ments. They's no real business with them. Ain't got no brains, them darkies. They can't deal in money. They just make

170

ar-range-ments." He spits in the road. Tobacco spit. It smells good, though it looks like something unmentionable. "Y'all the same, boy? No brains?"

No, sir, I'm thinking. You're the one with no brains. "If you want a melon, sir, I'll be happy to carry it home for you."

"What do I look like, a girlie? Hand me a melon."

"How about the biggest one, sir?" I say, polite as can be.

Mr. Johnson looks pleased. "That's right. The biggest one."

"That'll be twenty cents, sir." I dare to look directly in his face, searching for a reaction.

He pays his twenty cents and spits again.

"And remember, sir," I say, "they're selling *limoncello* today at Francesco Difatta's grocery."

"Lemon what?"

"You drink it cold. It's good on a hot day."

"Like today. It's hotter than the gates of hell today."

"Yes, sir. Francesco makes it himself. It takes your mind off your problems."

"Liquor? Wait'll John hears about this. You people. Never in my born days have I seen the likes. Selling liquor without a permit. No telling what y'all be up to next." He walks off with the melon.

"Twenty cents," says Cirone in Sicilian. "He's going to be burning angry when he finds out everyone else got a melon for fifteen."

What I did is a lot worse than overcharging Mr. Coleman for the strawberries. There's no way Mr. Coleman could know I overcharged. Besides, it was only a penny. But this was a whole nickel, and everyone else knows the price. I must have lost my mind. I wipe sweat from my neck. "Anyway, he got the biggest one."

We work our way back and forth across town from north to south, till we finish. There are only four melons left. And a pile of sweet potatoes.

I climb up on the bench beside Giuseppe. "We got no one to sell the rest to. And we can't eat them all." I clear my throat. "I know some families that could use a watermelon."

"Yeah?" Giuseppe tightens the reins. "Are we driving by the church?"

"I'll take one to their home. There's no road out there. I'll walk."

"Cirone, you go, too," says Giuseppe.

"I can carry a melon myself."

"You can carry two if there are two of you," says Giuseppe. "And take them those nasty orange things."

"No, I want sweet potato pies," I say.

"Carlo doesn't know how to make sweet potato pies."

"I'll make them."

"You?" Giuseppe shrugs.

And so Giuseppe drives across South Street and lets us off near the bayou. Cirone and I walk the grassy path to Patricia's house with the melons.

"You know, I can carry two melons myself," I say.

"No, you can't," says Cirone.

"Yes, I can."

"If Charles is there, I'll talk to him. If not, I'll just leave the melon and go. You can talk to Patricia alone."

"That isn't what I meant."

"Ha!"

We walk in silence.

"Did she like the bowl?" asks Cirone.

"Yes."

"I knew she would."

Finally, we get there. I go up on the porch and knock my elbow on the open door.

A woman stands by a pot-bellied stove, where an iron's heating up on top. Long face, long arms, long fingers. A pile of ironed and folded laundry sits on the foot of a bed. There's a sewing machine in the corner. She looks up at us and fear crumples her forehead. She rushes to the door. Cirone and I step back as she comes out on the porch. She looks around, then back at us. "Y'all alone?"

"Yes, ma'am."

She blinks. "Anybody see y'all come up here?"

"Ain't nobody to see us," says Cirone. "Ma'am." The houses out here are scattered through the trees. You can't see more than one at a time except in winter.

She wipes the sweat from her brow. "Well, come on in quick." She gives a small smile as we pass by, and closes the door behind us. She walks over and picks up the iron, spatters water on a shirt on the table, and sets that iron down on it with a hiss. She irons the shirt, folds it, and puts it on the pile. "Boys?"

"Yes, ma'am?"

"Mr. Blander—you know who he is?"

"Yes, ma'am."

"A smart man, Mr. Blander. He warned my sister. Said it ain't a good idea for you to come visiting here. At our house."

How did Blander guess we'd come here? Maybe the whole town's guessing about us. "We got watermelons."

"I can see that."

"We're delivering melons. Like we delivered them all over town."

She smiles at us for real this time. "Blander ain't the only smart one." She's sweating so much, her dress is all soppy at the neck. "Want to set them melons down? On the floor will be fine. Till I finish this ironing." She irons a pillowcase and folds it. Then she takes a towel and wipes her face and neck. "What can I do for y'all?"

"Are you Patricia's mother?" I ask, but her smile gave her away. And her eyes.

"Yes."

"I'm Calogero."

"I'm Cirone," says Cirone.

"I figured. Nice to finally meet y'all. Thought I'd meet you at the graduation party."

"It was a good party," says Cirone.

"Thank you."

"You're good at ironing," I say.

She laughs. "This is my sister's job. She iron up at the Blander house. But she took to bed sick, so here I am. This way she don't lose her job. But y'all don't want to hear about that. I expect you came to see my onliest boy, Charles, and my onliest girl, Patricia. They ain't here."

"We'll just leave these melons and go, then."

"Much obliged. Please tell your family that."

"I'll do that."

"Happy Fourth of July," says Cirone.

"Same to you," says Patricia's mother. "Y'all going to the festivities tomorrow?"

"What festivities?" I ask.

She gives an odd smile. "Well, there'll be some mighty big doings all over town, don't y'all know that? Specially at our church. The picnic will start in the late afternoon, after it cool off a bit." She blinks. "You know what? Your family ought to come. Brother Caleb will slaughter a hog. So if y'all come on over early, you two boys, I'll fry you up some brains and eggs."

I love brains. "What about what Blander said?"

"The church the Lord's house. I reckon no one going to say who can and can't come visiting in His house." Patricia's mother tilts her head. "They's going to be ice cold lemonade. And my lemon pie has two inches of calf slobbers on top."

"I'll tell my family," I say.

"Y'all do that."

We walk back along the path. Once we're out of hearing distance, Cirone says, "Why do you always have to act so stupid?"

"What'd I do stupid?"

"You acted like we don't know about the Fourth of July."

"I don't know about the Fourth of July."

"Well, I do," says Cirone. "Everyone in America does. I'm not the new one here. You are. Ask me about things before you go acting so dumb."

"How can I ask about things I don't know about?"

"Shut up."

We walk a ways, kicking the dirt.

"What's calf slobbers?"

Cirone laughs. "I knew you didn't follow that. Ha! It's meringue, dummy."

Back at the grocery John Wilson, the saloon keeper, is standing in the doorway.

I touch the tip of my cap. "Good day, Mr. Wilson."

Mr. Wilson smirks, but doesn't say a word. And doesn't move.

"Could we get by, please, sir?"

He moves aside.

Cirone and I slip past him.

"You open it?" Francesco's talking to old Pat Matthews, loud with anger. I'm surprised; we've always been on good terms with Pat. He makes himself useful doing odd jobs here and there. Francesco's hired him lots of times. We're all usually real gentle with him 'cause he's sick in the head from his war days. "Who tell you do that?"

"The box was sitting there," says Pat. "What's the harm? It ain't nothing personal. It just came off the train."

"Somebody tell you, eh? Somebody nose in my business? How much they pay you?" Francesco picks up the broom from behind the weighing counter. "You go back to Milliken's Bend." He chases Pat out the door.

Mr. Wilson moves aside obligingly as Pat passes. He turns to face into the store. "I can't hardly believe my eyes. If I ain't mistaken, you just chased a white man with a broom. And I ain't mistaken. Pat's old and broken-down with the drink and all—but he was a soldier. You either color blind or plum crazy."

"This trouble no concern you," says Francesco.

"Got troubles, huh? That's what you people attract: trouble." His upper lip curls at the words *you people*.

"You stand in doorway," says Francesco. "Fifteen minutes you stand there. Why?"

"So no one comes in."

"You block business."

"Now you got the idea." Mr. Wilson taps his temple. "You block my business, I block yours."

"I no understand."

"I just bet you no understand. Play dumb with me? Where's this lemon stuff you're thinking of selling?"

"Ah, I understand. You sell whisky. I no sell whisky."

"You bet your sorry ass you no sell whisky. It takes a permit to sell whisky. Y'all ain't got no permit."

"I no sell whisky."

"That's right. You got no permit. You got no government tax stamps. That's how it works in Louisiana. Ain't nothing like that country you come from. We regulate. Understand?"

"I no sell whisky."

"You sell one drop of that lemon stuff and I'll get Sheriff Lucas in here so fast, you won't have time to cock a gun."

"You see gun here? No gun here."

"Good."

"You want vegetable? Fruit?"

"No."

"Then you leave my store."

"If I hear . . ."

"I no sell whisky."

"You got the chorus right. Go back to your goats now. Drink that stinky milk. Eat that rotten cheese. Use just one barrel of flour to make miles of that crap you eat—those wormy strands. Don't buy nothing from nobody. That's fine. We don't need your money. We can get through these hard times without dirty money from dirty foreigners. But listen good." He points a finger at Francesco's nose. "Ain't that much business these days—and ain't no one going to stand for you stealing theirs."

"Goodbye, Mr. Wilson."

Mr. Wilson leaves.

Francesco turns to us. "Never go in his saloon," he shouts in Sicilian.

"We don't go in saloons," I say.

"Don't talk back to me." He slams his hand on the weighing counter. "Get to work. We have to fill the pint bottles with *limoncello*. It's business time."

"You just promised Mr. Wilson you wouldn't sell it," says Cirone.

"I promised I wouldn't sell whisky. *Limoncello* isn't whisky. And I've already got orders for almost all of it. Get to work."

"I've got to go mail my present for Rocco," I say.

Francesco looks at me. "All right. We agreed on that. But hurry."

eighteen

"We're not Protestants." Carlo chops potatoes on the big board.

I'm standing beside him, peeling onions. Rosario sits with his elbows on the table and his head in his hands. Francesco and Giuseppe are out on the porch talking. We have to hurry, Cirone and me. We have to get Carlo and Rosario on our side before Francesco comes in. It's already afternoon. The Fourth of July is going to pass us by.

"It's a birthday party," says Cirone. "The birthday party of this country. It has nothing to do with religion."

"Then why is it at a church?" says Carlo.

"The graduation party was at the church," Cirone says. "And we went to that."

Good for him. He's getting good at arguing.

"That was different," says Carlo. "That was the school's party."

"This is the country's party."

"Stop!" Rosario looks up. His eyelids droop as if he's got a headache. "We're not going to that church."

"We went there before," says Cirone. "And we had a good time."

"Stop!" This time it's Francesco. He comes into the room and takes a seat. Giuseppe's right behind him.

"Onions." Carlo holds out his hand.

I push two peeled onions toward him and work on a third.

"We were just talking about the Fourth of July," says Cirone in a reasonable tone.

"I know exactly what you were talking about," says Francesco. "We're not going to the Protestant church."

"The American birthday party," says Cirone. "That's all it is. And we're Americans."

"I'm not," says Giuseppe. "And neither are you two boys."

"It's a picnic," says Cirone.

"You want a picnic?" says Carlo. "I'm making a *frittata*."

"No," says Cirone. "They don't eat *frittata* at a picnic. They eat—"

"Stop!" Francesco slaps the table. "You heard Carlo."

"Besides," says Carlo, "we're having our own party."

"We can't have our own party on the Fourth of July," says Cirone. "It's an American party—it's got to be at an American place."

I'm stunned. Cirone's never acted like this. Downright belligerent.

"I didn't mean today," says Carlo. "Next Saturday is July fifteenth. Perfect for the *festa* of Santa Rosalia. A good Catholic celebration."

"We can't do a *festa* then," says Rosario. "That's the day of the town ball and tournament. We'll have lots of extra work."

"Right," says Francesco. "We'll postpone a week. Santa Rosalia won't mind."

"Beppe and Salvatore always come," says Carlo. "Someone's got to tell them."

I perk up in spite of myself. "I'll go to Milliken's Bend." Beppe and Salvatore are the only other Sicilians in this part of Louisiana; just being around them makes all of us happy. Beppe is married to the sister of Francesco and Giuseppe and Carlo. She's back in Cefalù. Salvatore is Beppe's son. He's ten years old. All through the winter we saw them every Saturday, but now we haven't seen them since before spring planting.

"Look at all you," Cirone bursts out. He puts his hands together as if in prayer and shakes them furiously at Carlo and Francesco and all of them. "You don't get excited at a Fourth of July festival—a huge thing—but you jump with joy at some dumb saint's *festa*. You act like we're still back in Sicily."

"We don't forget the saints," says Carlo. "No matter where we are."

Giuseppe walks toward Cirone, glaring. "And we never forget we're Sicilian."

"All right, all right," says Rosario. He steps in front of Cirone. "That's settled. Carlo's making a picnic. Let's all help."

And so we carry a table out near the edge of the woods and we spread a tablecloth on it and set out the plates and forks and knives and spoons. We eat *frittata* under the broiling sun. And hot watermelon.

"I hate this," whispers Cirone to me in English.

"Frittata?" I whisper back. "What's wrong with *frittata?"*

"They call it omelet here."

"Omelet?"

"It's a French word. From New Orleans. French is better than Sicilian." He blows through his lips in disgust. "This ain't how it's done in America."

"How's it done?"

"Barbecue. You got to see for yourself." Cirone stands up. "Can we go get ice cream?" he says loudly in Sicilian to no one in particular.

"We've got cold *limoncello* back at the house," says Carlo.

"Ice cream is what you eat on the Fourth of July," says Cirone.

"Like you know all about it," says Rosario.

"My friends told me."

And I'm scanning my memory. Charles and Ben and Rock—they never said anything about ice cream in front of me. What's Cirone talking about?

"Ice cream would go down easy in this heat," says Francesco. "I'd like some."

"No, I mean just Calogero and me. Can we go? It's a holiday for everyone in the whole country. Let us go get ice cream."

"Go on," says Francesco. "Here." He takes a nickel out of his pocket. "Have fun. And bring back a penny."

I take the nickel.

Cirone glances at me sideways. But I don't get why.

We walk toward town. There's music coming from somewhere near Depot Street. But once we're out of sight of the men, Cirone turns off the path.

"Where are you going?"

"The church," says Cirone in English. "The ice cream saloon is closed, anyway. Everything closes on the Fourth of July."

"You'll get in trouble with Rosario," I answer in English. "And I'll get in worse trouble with Francesco."

"They told us to go have fun. They didn't tell us not to go to the church."

"Are you crazy? We both know what they meant. And they know we know it. Besides, you said we were going for ice cream."

"There'll be ice cream at the church. All we have to do is eat some and we can answer—we went out for ice cream." Cirone looks at me in disgust. "By the way, Mister Pocket-the-Money, what happened to the four pennies Francesco gave us last time?"

"I spent them."

"On what?"

"Postage. I didn't think it would be that much. I sent a birthday present to Rocco. I'm sorry. You can have the four cents this time."

"You don't tell anyone we went to the church, and we can share these four cents."

"All right." My heart is beating hard. "Maybe we should bring something."

Cirone stops. "Like what?"

"We didn't sell all the *limoncello* pints yesterday."

"Good thinking."

We turn again and go to the grocery. It's locked, of course. But it's easy to get in through the high rear window. I give Cirone a boost and he's up and inside fast.

"Here." He holds a pint out the window.

I take it.

"Here." He holds out another.

I take it.

"Here."

"Francesco will notice. Two's enough."

"Just take it."

I do.

He climbs to the window and jumps out onto the ground.

I look around. "We can't walk through town with bottles in our hands."

Cirone takes off his shirt and wraps them in it. "It's too hot for a shirt, anyway."

Nee-haw. Bedda peeks around the grocery corner and bolts over to greet us.

"You are such a bother." I push Bedda in the side. "Go on home."

We walk and she follows.

"Don't look back," I say. "She'll go away if we don't look at her."

But she doesn't go away.

"We can't go to a picnic with a goat. Here, hold these." Cirone hands me the bundle of *limoncello* pints. He races at Bedda shouting, "*Via, via*–away!"

"Well, look who's here." Three boys come down the street. It's the bullies. The one who just spoke is the one who kicked my cap from my hand.

"With a goat this time."

"She's probably their girlfriend."

They laugh.

Cirone backs up till he's half behind me.

Bedda follows him, but the tallest bully quick catches her around the neck. She bucks. He's big and strong, though; he holds on. "Want your girlfriend back, boys?"

"What are you ready to do to get your girlfriend back? Huh?" says another bully. "Y'all going to shoot us?"

"Yeah. We know about that noisy one. The liar who runs the grocery store. He shot a little darkie boy just for stealing a watermelon."

They've got it all wrong. Francesco didn't shoot Jerome the Thief. Giuseppe just went "bang" with his finger.

"And that other one—the one who don't speak any English at all. He shot the old soldier from Milliken's Bend. He shot a white man!"

Who's spreading these lies?

"No gun today, boys?" says the one holding Bedda. "Well, if you want her back, you got to pay. You got money?" His arms are around her neck. Will he strangle her?

I put my hand in my pocket.

"Whoa!" shouts one of the boys. "Stop right there. You chunk a rock at us and y'all'll be sorry. We'll pitch a fight you ain't never going to forget."

I slowly take the nickel out of my pocket and roll it in the street.

The tall bully's eyes go wide. He lets go of Bedda and chases the nickel.

We run, Cirone and Bedda and me. When I look back, they're gone.

"That was dumb," says Cirone in English. "Now they'll try to get money off us all the time. And we ain't got a penny to give back to Francesco. Dumb!"

"What would you have done?"

"Same dumb thing you did."

I laugh, but I'm not happy. "I'll tell Francesco I lost the penny."

"Good."

"If you tell him you stole the *limoncello*."

Cirone spits in the street. "He ain't going to notice the *limoncello*. Stop whining."

I'm just jittery because of those bullies. "Why are we speaking English?"

"I'm sick of being Italian, Calogero. I been thinking about it since you read me those newspapers. I been remembering. I can't stand being different. I can't stand it no more. I've gone my whole life without friends because I was afraid." He looks down. His bottom lip trembles just the slightest.

All those years before I came, Cirone had no one. I swallow and throw my arm across his skinny bare shoulders.

He shrugs me off and looks me in the face. "Rosario and Carlo and Francesco and Giuseppe, they were like a wall around me. Well, I ain't staying inside no wall no more. I'm different now. I got friends. And I don't care who beats me up—I'm keeping them. I'm speaking English outside the house."

"All right. Me too."

"I'm going to eat American food every chance I get."

I love Sicilian food. But this is important. "Me too."

"I'm going to act American. I'll become an American citizen."

"Maybe I will, too."

Music comes from ahead, from the direction of Patricia's church. A brass band.

"We can't take Bedda to the church," I say.

"We go back home now and we ain't never going to get out again."

I take off my shirt without unbuttoning it and slip it over Bedda's head so that it hangs around her neck. Then I grab on to the shirt so that I've got her tight. The buttons won't hold if she fights me. I pet her, to calm her.

Cirone laughs. "The both of us, half naked. What do you think they'll do?"

"Guess we'll find out." I grin.

The church lawn is filled with people again. Some are at tables. Others have spread tablecloths on the grass and they're sitting right there on the ground, eating. Some aren't even using forks. Just picking up food with their fingers and talking and laughing.

"Now that's a barbecue," says Cirone. "This is America. Let's be all-American for one afternoon."

Patricia walks up the road as though she's been on the lookout. There're ribbons in her hair. Red, white, and blue, like the flag. Her legs stick out from under that old flowered dress, strong in the sunlight. I will be American for this girl. I will be anything she wants me to be.

"You sure jar my preserves."

"What are you talking about?" I ask.

She laughs. "You came. No shirt. And a goat. But you came." And she smiles.

Cirone unwraps the *limoncello* pints. "These are for your family. But you got to put them in the icebox before you drink them."

Patricia gapes at the bottles. "Liquor? Y'all crazy? Can't bring no liquor to church."

Cirone shrugs. "We ain't got nothing else to bring."

"Y'all already done contributed two melons. But come on, follow me." She leads us along the road and around to the far side of the church. There's a rose trellis running half the length of the wall, covered with red blossoms so thick it looks like a green and red blanket. She disappears behind it and sticks out her hand. "Gimme."

Patricia stashes those three pints somewhere behind the roses.

Cirone puts on his shirt. "Where're the boys?"

"Follow the food smell and you'll find them for sure."

Cirone sniffs loudly and grins. "See you later." He takes off.

Patricia puts out her hand again.

I go behind the rose trellis.

The dim air hangs dense with rose perfume. It makes me woozy.

Patricia takes the ribbons from her hair. She ties them

together in a long string. Then she takes my shirt off Bedda and she ties Bedda to the trellis with her ribbons.

I put on my shirt and peer at her in the shady dark. I don't know what to say. "How do you make sweet potato pies?"

She laughs. "Roast the biggest ones in the fire. Then peel them and squish them and add chopped pecans. And butter, if y'all got it. If not, milk. If not, it don't matter. And sugar. Or, if you like the taste, molasses. Or skip it. Only thing matter is the pecans. Then put it all in a baked pie shell and stick it in the oven. Easy."

"Much obliged."

"So that's how it is?"

"That's how what is?"

"Ain't you going to kiss me hello?"

And I do.

"Want to go out to the party?" she asks.

"No. I want to stay here, with you."

She laughs, again. "Too bad for you." And she leads me out to my first American Fourth of July.

nineteen

A few days later Patricia and I are walking the clay road to Milliken's Bend. Both of us have errands there. Her feet move quick. "If anyone come, you go off the right side," she says. "I go left."

"Why?"

She lets out a whistle. "You something else, all right. For a murderer you sure don't know nothing."

My cheeks sting as if I've been smacked. "Don't you say that."

"Say what?"

"That I'm a murderer."

"All Eye-talian men murderers." She laughs.

"How can you laugh? I told you about those newspapers to make you understand. It's the worst lie I ever heard."

"It ain't no worse than saying all colored men rapists."

I stop. "Your uncles and brother and Rock and Ben— they'd go crazy if they heard you say that."

"Mortified." Patricia looks back at me, but she doesn't stop walking.

"What's that mean?"

"How they'd feel. Mortified. Like you want to die. Like you felt when you read those newspapers. But it's the truth. The plantation owners' truth. And if you don't learn to respect that truth, you done for."

"Respect a lie?"

"A lie they believe . . . well, Calogero, that kind of lie can kill you. Really kill you. Not just mortify you."

"Murderers." I run to catch up. "It drives me crazy that they believe that. That's why they can start that stupid rumor that my uncles shot an old man and some little kid."

"Just 'cause that drunk soldier wobbled out of the grocery on his own two feet and because that little loud-mouth thief, Jerome, go around bragging he got a bellyache from eating your watermelon—you mean because of that it's a lie? Don't be dumb, Calogero. Them facts don't change nothing. You listen to me. Anybody come along this road, you dive to the right, I go to the left. Get out of sight fast. And if they stop, run."

"It's barely daylight. Who's going to come?"

"Just dive. And hide."

"What would they do if we didn't hide?"

"An Eye-talian boy and a colored girl? Y'all crazy?"

"Sicilians have Negro girlfriends in New Orleans. My uncle told me."

"Well, this ain't New Orleans. And I hope you never find out how this place act."

I think of Dago Joe. I didn't tell Patricia about him. "I'm going to find out. You're my girl."

"Oh, so you kissed me and now you think you own me?"

"I didn't mean it that way."

"You meant my heart, huh? Well, I'm hanging on to my heart a while longer."

I want to say my heart is hers. But it doesn't seem right after what she just said. I look up and down the road. No one's coming. "Should we walk through the fields?"

"Five miles to Milliken's Bend. And so hot, the trees be bribing the dogs for a shower. Any other path will take longer. Walk fast and stop moaning."

"I ain't moaning."

"Listen to that: 'I ain't moaning.' " She sashays in front of me. "You talked normal for once. Not like some school-teacher."

"Frank Raymond."

"Right, he yours. But Miss Clarrie, she a teacher, too. And y'all talk the same. She from somewhere far away. New Jersey. You want to hear her talk?"

"You bet I would."

"Well, Mr. Calogero," says Patricia in a pinched, formal voice. She stretches her neck long, so her head seems to wobble on top of it. "That is your name, isn't it, young man? Did I hear right? I'm delighted to meet you. To what do I owe the pleasure of your visit? Could I offer you something? Perhaps a cool drink of lemonade?"

I laugh. "I thought you meant really meet her."

She looks at me sideways. "After I get all the aprons and dresses from my cousin, after you see your friends, we'll visit Miss Clarrie. She live in Milliken's Bend."

"Really?"

"Mmm-hmm. She ain't no fancy lady. Just a smart one. Hurry now. We got to beat the sun. And keep your eyes open."

I look up and down the road again.

"No, not that. Look to either side as we come up on this field."

The road goes straight through cotton fields. The tiny plants have grown a lot since the last time I passed here. They're bushy with vivid green leaves, broad and shiny.

"Stop," says Patricia. "Stop and watch."

The sun hits the fields gradually, and it shines white up

here, pink over there, crimson beyond. The next instant the whole place sparkles white and pink and crimson all at once. Flowers! They open with the sunlight. So many of them. And those blossoms, they actually glow.

"You playing 'gator?" asks Patricia.

"What?"

"You standing there with your mouth open like a 'gator catching flies."

I shake my head. "I was just looking at the flowers. They're waking up."

"See why we came at dawn? Ain't they the best?"

"The best, all right. But why are there three kinds?"

"The flower come out white, then the next day it open pink, then the next day red, then it fall off. All in three days. Next week the flowers will be gone. And last week, wasn't hardly any. That's why I waited till now to go to Milliken's Bend."

"That why you invited me to come along?"

"Company make sense, seeing as we going the same place." She lifts her chin and turns me a smooth cheek, but I can tell I caught her. I imagine touching her cheeks.

"They look like silk feels," I say.

"Them flowers? You ever touched silk?"

"My mother had a silk shawl that belonged to her mother. Mamma was from Rome—how she ever wound up in Sicily, I don't know. Anyway, she had this shawl in a box and once, when I was little, she wrapped me in it. I remember how it made me feel."

She stops. "Wait here." She runs into the field, disappearing between two rows.

I watch up and down the street. A wagon's coming. I duck down the row she went in. "Patricia? Patricia? Where are you? There's a wagon on the road. Stay hidden." I flatten myself on the ground with my chin on the dirt and watch the narrow span of road I can see between the plant rows.

Patricia wriggles up beside me. "You fool," she whispers. "I told you to dive to the other side. Now if they come after us, they don't have to bust up."

Come after us? We didn't do anything.

It seems like forever for that wagon to get here. It rolls on by. Men. I can't see how many. Crates piled high. Gone. I get to my knees.

Patricia pulls me back down. "Stay put awhile. Let it get a good distance away. Here." She shoves something into my hand.

It's a deep brown husk with an almond-colored inside. "What is this?"

"The outside of a cotton boll. Old, from last autumn. They's tons of them on the ground. Dig around. But most fall apart, beaten up by the winter. This one whole. Feel inside. Feel the lining."

I run my thumb inside the cotton-boll husk. "It's so soft."

"Like silk."

"Like you." I kiss her cheek.

197

She pushes me away, then stands and checks the road. "Time to go."

We walk. "Charles told me he chops cotton in autumn," I say.

"For Mr. Coleman." She says it with a sneer.

"You don't like him?"

"His soul fell out of the ugly tree and hit every branch on the way down."

"That's how I feel about him, too." I go tight all over, just thinking about how Mr. Coleman acted in the grocery when we didn't wait on him first.

"Why you talking about Charles chopping cotton, anyway?"

"I want to chop cotton, too."

"Whites don't chop cotton."

"Sicilians aren't white. Ask Sheriff Lucas."

"Eye-talian." She closes her lips in a smile that makes her cheeks bulge like big sweet onions. "But Eye-talian ain't the same as colored."

"Then I'm nothing. So no dumb law says I can't chop cotton."

"White folks' heads full of rules ain't never been writ down as law."

"Well, they can't have it both ways. They can't block me from white things and Negro things at the same time. I want to chop cotton, so I'm going to chop cotton."

"Ain't you bold. And foolish. Listen here, Calogero.

Cotton bolls stick to your fingers. And you got to bend a million times, so your back and neck hurt."

"But it's beautiful," I say. "I want to work in the cotton fields. Italians work on the plantations down near New Orleans."

"Ain't no one ever seen no Eye-talian chopping cotton here. But maybe they hire you. Maybe." Patricia pulls a little cylinder wrapped in paper from her pocket. She unwraps it, pulls it into two pieces, and hands me one. "Eat real slow."

I look at her. She chews her half. I stick it in my mouth. It's soft and chocolatey and chewy. "Yum."

"Slow," she says. "Ain't no more where that came from."

I make it last as long as I can.

"Tootsie," says Patricia. "The name of the candy."

"Did you buy it in the penny-candy store in Tallulah?"

"Y'all crazy? Only boys 'llowed in there—white boys. And y'all better put on a cap and knickerbockers even if you stand outside and ask to buy at the back window."

"So Charles bought it for you?"

"Where Charles going to get knickerbockers?"

"All right," I say. "How'd you get this candy?"

"Miss Clarrie. She visited New York City last summer. A store run by a Mr. Hirshfield. And Mr. Hirshfield got a daughter go by the nickname Tootsie. She like these candies, so they got her name now." She runs her tongue over her top teeth. "Miss Clarrie gave five to each of us for Christmas. I been eating mine slow."

"And you shared the last one with me." So she didn't mean what she said about her heart, after all. I move close to her. "Thank you."

She pushes me away. "Don't mention it."

Why is it this girl brings up kisses all on her own sometimes and other times pushes me away? I feel half crazy. I want to run. So I do. I run a circle around her.

She doesn't even look at me.

In the distance the plantation bells ring. People are waking for work.

The road follows a bayou on one side now, and a ditch on the other, with a meadow beyond. I look up and down the road and panic flickers in me. "Where can we hide if someone comes along?"

"Behind the first cypress you reach. Ain't no one going to come after you in a swamp 'cause of the 'gators. 'Less they on the hunt for you anyway."

"Are there really 'gators in this little swamp?"

" 'Gators in every swamp, Calogero."

I flinch. "Sicilians don't go in swamps."

"Oh yeah? I heard different. I heard you acted pretty brave in the skiff."

"That was before I knew what was going on. I have a confession. I hate 'gators. I mean, I love eating them. I love the way you make them. But hunting them?" I shiver.

She laughs. "They's worse things than 'gators, Calogero. At least a 'gator stay in the swamp and don't get you by surprise. When you dealing with a 'gator, you know who you dealing with."

I think of Joseph, talking about 'gators. He said they were honest. That's sort of like what Patricia's saying. But I don't want to think about 'gators now. I'm spending the day with Patricia. With my girl. I sneeze.

"Do plants make you sneeze?" She points. "The tall purple flowers on the ditch bank, they asters. They don't bother nobody. But them others, they goldenrod. Lots of people sneeze at them."

"You know plants, too, besides birds."

"Just the plants I like."

We walk fast. And soon we're past the bayou and between cotton fields again. A fat bird and her chicks are pecking by the roadside. "Partridge," says Patricia.

Then the road passes through woodland with a ditch bank on both sides now. It's cooler in this stretch of shade. Pine scents the air. Squirrels race chattering through the ferns and up a trunk. "You like squirrel stew?" asks Patricia.

"I never had it. But if you made it, I would."

She laughs.

"I mean it."

"Well, I know that."

The towns ahead and behind are clearly awake now, because lots of people pass on the road, and we're ducking behind trees every few minutes.

A bird calls. "A warbler," says Patricia. "Ain't too many of them around here. Oh, hear that? A bobwhite. Good eating. Plenty of them over by the levee in the blackberry canes." She laughs. "I said too much. I'm showing off. 'Cause of your smooth talk."

"I love blackberries. I'll go picking with you."

"Oh no you won't. Not over there. I ain't never seen such a sight of chiggers as Charles had when he got done blackberry picking there last season."

"What are chiggers?"

She laughs. "A boy who don't know about chiggers, well, that boy blessed. And I ain't going to unbless you. Wild coffee grow by the levee, too."

"Does it taste good?"

"Sometimes on a Friday when the money gone and there ain't no more till we get paid after sundown Saturday, we run out of regular coffee, and my mamma will make a pot from a single bean. Like tan water. So it's good to have wild coffee beans, too."

I love the way she talks. "I could listen to you all day."

"Ha! You saying I talk too much?"

"No. Not at all. I'm serious."

And so we chatter all the way to Milliken's Bend.

twenty

We stop at the edge of town. "Should we go to Miss Clarrie's now?" I ask.

"Business first."

"Then I'll meet you in a half hour," I say. "Is that all right?"

"No, sir, it is not all right. I want to go in every shop that say I can, and for them that don't, I want to window-shop."

"I'll window-shop with you."

"No, sir, you will not. Don't act like a booger that you

can't thump off. We will not be caught together. If we pass one another, we can say, 'Good day.' I'll see you at Miss Clarrie's at eleven. Listen for the church bell. Her house up the road behind the church, way way up and to the right. They's a birdbath out front."

And she runs off.

I walk down the business side of the main street of Milliken's Bend. All the homes are on the other side, neat and orderly. They've got gardens and shrubs out front and trees with purple blossoms and wide, waxy leaves. A chicken's pecking in the flower bed over there, clucking nonstop. This is the prettiest town ever.

The smell of teas and spices and coffee makes me stop in front of the first open shop door. But I don't dare go in, because I saw Patricia enter. She told me to stay away from her. A man sits on a chair on the sidewalk whittling soft driftwood with a butcher knife. He's making a toy horse. Rocco would love that. If I had pennies on me, I'd buy it for him. I can almost hear his squeal of delight. I blink back tears. The man looks at me, then looks down again, but it's not unfriendly. Just quiet.

The next store smells like tobacco. A sign says the man will roll a cigar for three cents. Francesco rolls our cigars himself, but the ones in the window look tighter. Maybe they're better. Maybe once I get my hands on some pennies again, I'll buy Francesco a store-rolled cigar, too.

I enter the third store. "Calogero!" Salvatore races over

and we hug and dance around the grocery store. "It's been so long. I miss you. How's Cirone? Come on into the back and see Papà." He pulls me into the rear of the store.

"Calogero!" Beppe puts down a crate and runs to me. We hug and he slaps my back. "You look good," he says in Sicilian. "And how're my brothers-in-law?"

"Everyone's fine. You look good, too."

"Business is good. Almost no one around Milliken's Bend shops at the plantation stores anymore. They know they get better fruits and vegetables at better prices from me." Beppe's strutting just like Francesco; I can't help but smile. "And if they can't afford it, well, we figure something out. Come with me, so you can see for yourself." He leads me out onto the front sidewalk and points. "A man with a family of four children, he put new shingles up on this roof. See how good they look? When it rains, not a drop, not one single drop comes through. So I'll feed his family for the winter months, when there's hardly any work. Good business, right? And with other people I trade other things. Yesterday I ate hominy with black molasses. Have you tried that?"

I shake my head.

"Not bad. Not good like spaghetti. But not bad." He touches his lip in memory.

"Hello, Beppe," comes a voice in English.

We turn to see a well-dressed man. He gives a quick smile.

"Ah, Mr. Ward. A pleasure," says Beppe in passable English.

"My wife ain't feeling well. She asked me to pick up a few things."

"Not feeling well? Sorry. Sorry, sorry. You come. We choose sweet things. You take home chamomile. Boil it. Make tea. Then she feel better. You see." Beppe goes back in the store with Mr. Ward.

I stay out on the sidewalk with Salvatore.

Patricia comes out of the tobacco store. What was she doing in there all this time? She sees me and walks on past with "Good day, Calogero."

"Good day, Patricia."

"Good day, Patricia," echoes Salvatore in my ear. And his English sounds just like anyone's. No accent.

I watch Patricia from the back as she turns into the next store. She doesn't give me a second glance, but I know she feels my eyes on her. My arms and chest get warm.

"You in love with her?" asks Salvatore in English.

Well, I deserve that, gaping after Patricia like a fool. I turn to face Salvatore. "You're too little to ask that."

"I may be ten, but I ain't stupid. And you ain't stupid, neither; she's pretty."

"She's beautiful."

When Mr. Ward leaves the store, Salvatore and I go inside again.

"I came to invite you to the *festa* of Santa Rosalia," I say in Sicilian to Beppe.

206

"Saturday," he says. "Like every year. I'm counting on it."

"Only we have to do it late this year. A week from Saturday, on the twenty-second. You'll still come, right?"

"Of course." Beppe claps his hands together and shakes them happily. "I'll bring my accordion. We'll stay the night, singing and dancing till the stars go to bed."

"Sounds good," I say. "All right, then." I turn to go.

"You're not leaving! You walked all this way. Stay for midday dinner at least."

"I've got things I have to do."

"He's in love," says Salvatore.

"In love?" Beppe pushes his lips forward.

"Salvatore's just being dumb."

"In love." Beppe pulls a stool out from behind the weighing counter. He sits and looks thoughtful. "I've got to bring my Concetta here. I miss her so much."

"I hardly remember Mamma," says Salvatore.

"Don't say that. Don't you ever say that."

I shake my head. "If business is going good, how come you can't send for her?"

"It's not the money. I send her money every month. She doesn't come because she's afraid of the South. Back home they hear stories about America—she knows more about what happens to Sicilians here than I do. She says I should move to New York City. They're going to build an underground railway system and they want men who know how to make tunnels. No one in the world makes better tunnels than Italians."

"Maybe you should go."

"I grow vegetables, Calogero. I trade them, I sell them. I wouldn't know what to do digging underground. I wouldn't know who I was."

I look at Salvatore.

He's looking straight at me.

Is it worse to have a dead mother or a mother who's alive, but on the other side of the ocean?

"I've got to go." I give Salvatore a special hug, and go back into the bright sun. No sign of Patricia. But it can't be long till eleven. I might as well find Miss Clarrie's.

I walk to the church and up the road behind. There's the house with the birdbath out front. It's a tenant farmer's shack. It doesn't look good enough for a real teacher.

If she sees me hanging around out front, she might get scared I'm someone bad. So I walk up and down the dirt path. Past the shack that has a mule tied by the side. Past the shack that has a big old pig. Up and down, up and down.

The church bell rings and Patricia comes skipping up the path, like a little kid.

"Did you buy anything?" I ask.

"Well, naturally. I bought everything I saw. I got money galore." She laughs.

"Even if you did have money, you wouldn't want everything you saw," I say. "You wouldn't want cigars."

"Sure I would. My mamma got a silver brandy flask,

but she ain't never touched a drop. It's the having that matters."

"Patricia, is that you?" A woman stands under the front awning of the shack. It's hard to describe her. The best word might be *uneven*. One shoulder is lower than the other. One arm hangs lower. Even one eye is lower. She looks like she's melting, the right side sliding away faster than the left. She holds her floury hands away from her dress. And her hair is reddish and so wispy, it looks like someone's half erased it.

"Miss Clarrie, I brought a friend to meet you. Calogero."

"Hello, Mr. Calogero."

I come up and take my cap off. "Good day, Miss Clarrie."

She tilts her head, and now she's so off balance, I feel like she's going to fall. "To what do I owe the pleasure of this visit?" she says, the very same way Patricia said it out on the road this morning.

I don't know what to say.

"She asking why you here," Patricia whispers in my ear.

"I'm coming to your school in September," I blurt.

"You are?" says Miss Clarrie.

"You are?" says Patricia.

"That is, if you'll let me, Miss Clarrie."

"Oh, I will definitely let you, Mister . . . what was your name?"

209

"Scalise. Scalise, Calogero."

"Scalise is your first name?"

"Is it?" asks Patricia. Her fists are on her hips and one eyebrow is raised.

I realize my mistake. "I'm sorry. I said it like in Italy. My family name is Scalise. My given name is Calogero."

"Is it all right if I call you Calogero?"

"Yes, please."

"Were you born in Italy?"

"Sicily. I came to America last October, ma'am."

"His ship landed in New Orleans," says Patricia. "He came by hisself. To live with his uncles. He snuck on a freight train. All by hisself."

"Thank you for that information, Patricia." Miss Clarrie looks at me thoughtfully. "That must have been difficult. Terrifying, in fact." My cheeks burn in embarrassment. "You must be resourceful, Calogero. I will be happy to have you in my classroom."

"Thank you, ma'am."

"It's for me to thank you. With you I will now have twenty-one students, even if Patricia here makes the regrettable decision not to return. With that number I am guaranteed a salary of fifty dollars a month, instead of forty. So thank you, Calogero."

"You're sincerely welcome, ma'am."

"And so polite." She laughs. "I believe it will be a delight to have you regardless of the money. Have you had your vaccination?"

"I don't know what that is."

"It's an injection that protects you from smallpox. You'll have to go to a doctor and get that before you come to school."

"Yes, ma'am."

"And you have to use your right hand in school for all your letters and numbers. That's the law."

"I'm right-handed, ma'am."

"Good. In school you must behave properly."

"No spitballs," says Patricia. "No bending back other people's hands or fighting or banging them on the head."

"Thank you for explaining that, Patricia," says Miss Clarrie.

"I'll behave properly."

"Good. Do you know any letters?"

"I can read."

"That's even better. Oh my, I wish I had had you with me last summer." She taps a finger delicately on her cheek. "I'm trying to get to know this state, you see. So I'm visiting two new parishes every summer. And last summer I visited Tangipahoa Parish. Have you ever heard of it?"

"Yes, ma'am. Sicilians grow strawberries there. The best kind."

"That's right. There's a whole town of Sicilians there. All the signs are in Sicilian—even the street signs. I certainly could have used someone who reads Italian there."

"I read English, too. I've had a tutor all year."

"Would you mind reading for me?"

"No, ma'am."

"Follow me." She walks inside to a table where a thick book lies. "My hands are too floury. Just pick it up, would you, please?"

"Cheapest Supply House on Earth. Our trade reaches around the world." I read about watches, jewelry, sewing machines, saddles.

"That's enough, Calogero. You're quite proficient."

"You planning on buying any of them things?" asks Patricia.

"This is from 1894, when catalogues were free. Now they charge. So I don't have a new one. I don't even know if Sears, Roebuck carries these things. That's the name of the store: Sears, Roebuck. Someday I'm going to Chicago to visit that store. And other sights. They hosted a world's fair six years ago, and the pavilions are still up. Travel is important."

"Miss Clarrie gave postal cards to each of us graduates," Patricia says.

I look in confusion at Miss Clarrie.

"Patricia, would you open this drawer, please?"

Patricia opens the little drawer in the table, and hands me a postal card.

"Hey, it's already addressed. To you, Miss Clarrie," I say.

"Right. I encourage my graduates to travel. To the next town. The next parish, state, country. Anywhere you go, it's good for you. You see new ways and learn to appreciate them. Books carry you far, too. But actually experiencing somewhere, ah, that's quite different. The world would be a better place if everyone traveled. I want all my graduates to write to me from somewhere else and tell me what they've seen."

I carefully place the postal card back in the drawer.

Miss Clarrie smiles. "Do you have any questions about school for me?"

"What do I need to buy?"

"Not a thing. Show up the first day, and I'll give you a pencil and a tablet—a copybook."

"The school monitor will pass them out," says Patricia. "And at the end of the day, the monitor will collect them."

"Thank you, Patricia. Well, now, I'm in the middle of making biscuits. Would the two of you like to stay for biscuits with sausage gravy?"

twenty-one

We're standing out front of Miss Clarrie's house, full of biscuits and gravy. She already told us goodbye and shut the door behind us. I reach for the bundle wrapped in brown paper and tied with string. "I'll carry that satchel if you want."

"Nuh-uh. You drop it and you ain't the one to suffer." Patricia holds it close. "These aprons and white dresses going to let me and six other girls make money."

"Doing what?"

"Working as servers in the dining room on the steamship this Sunday."

"What steamship?"

She shakes her head. "Ain't you heard about the tournament and the ball?"

"Sure I have. My uncles ordered all kinds of food from New Orleans for it."

"The ball will be on a ship. I could tell Mr. Coleman you want a job in the kitchen. Washing dishes and stuff. You'd get to see everything."

Working for Mr. Coleman. The very idea makes my jaw clench. Still . . . "Will Charles be working in the kitchen?"

"And Rock. And Ben."

I can't fight that. "Then I want to work, too. And Cirone does, too."

"I'll try."

I step off the porch. Patricia doesn't follow. "What are you waiting for?"

"Everyone going to see us," she says.

"You dive to one side, I dive to the other. That's your rule, right?"

"That's easy before dawn. They's too many folks out now. Besides, I can't go diving without getting this package all dirty. And look at that sky. Rain, for sure."

Charcoal gray clouds billow in from the north. "So what do you want to do?"

"Stash away till evening." She looks up and down the path. "Wait five minutes, then follow me."

"Five minutes? You'll be way ahead of me. How will I find you?"

"The good Lord gave you eyes, sugar." Patricia walks up the path, just as fast with that bundle as she was without it. I wonder what makes her that strong.

I count to sixty, five times. Then I'm off, up that path. Patricia's out of sight. I knew it. I can't even call for her; she'd only get mad. I walk, looking every which way. Soon the houses stop and the grasses grow tall. If there's a path, I can't see it. Hot wind pushes at my back, and it goes dark. Lightning. Thunder claps. Where is that girl?

Patricia steps out from a stand of woods ahead. She waves me on.

I run and now we're running together through the forest undergrowth. A furry, stub-faced, squat creature zips across in front of us. It races at a rabbit, hugs it, bites its head, and scratches at its belly with its hind feet, shredding it.

"Don't watch." Patricia runs on.

"What was that?"

"A mink. The thunder must have woke him. Usually you don't see them till dusk. But they's a pond near here. They live near ponds."

A shiver shoots through me. "Mean creature."

"I reckon he'll get his—a coyote or red wolf will eat him if a 'gator don't."

We dodge in and out of the trees until we come out on a field. A shabby building sits in the middle.

"Hurry."

Big fat drops are already falling. We run flat out for

the building and duck inside the front door just as it starts to pour.

It takes a while for my eyes to adjust to the shadows. Patricia puts her package in a dark corner, then comes over to stand beside me. "Lucky us. We just made it."

"Where are we?"

"This is an old cotton gin. That there . . ." She points. "That's the old boiler. And that's the gin stand." She walks to the wall. "Follow me." She climbs the wall holding on to nothing but those rough logs, all the way up to a loft. "Come on."

It isn't as hard as it looked. I'm up there with her quick. Straw pads the floor except for a spot in the middle that's been swept. "Who comes here?"

"Men. They play craps. Coloreds ain't allowed to gamble. But on Saturday night, people have to. Late tonight they be coming here, bet on that."

"How do you know about all this?"

"Everybody know."

The rain drums on the tin roof. I walk to the end of the loft and look out the open gable end. "It's coming down hard."

"Better for napping." She lies on the straw. I stretch out near her. "You really going to school in September?" asks Patricia.

"Mmm-hmm," I say, mimicking her. "You sure you're not going back with me?"

"I'm sure."

"Will you work for rich people in some big house?"

"Ain't enough rich people to go around, Calogero."

"So you'll work the cotton fields?"

"You got to chop two hundred pounds by midafternoon, then carry it to the gin—the running gin, not this old place—to get them tenacious seeds removed."

"Tenacious seeds?"

"That's what my uncle call them. They stick."

"I bet you're strong enough to do all that," I say.

"Thing is, you get old and tired overnight. And skinny. I like fat better. I'd rather shake than rattle, any day. I don't know what I'll do, but I'll find work."

The noise of the rain outside seals us in. I roll on my side and look at her. "What's school like?"

"Beatings ain't allowed. The last teacher, though, she smacked us with her ruler."

"Did she get fired for it?"

"Ain't nobody told on her. If you told, your folks would whip you for misbehaving in school—hurt you a lot worse than a smack from a ruler. But Miss Clarrie, she'll give you a bawling out, oh, yes, but she ain't never hit nobody."

"What else?"

"Well, you'll see. The most important thing, though, is love your teacher."

"Love her? How come?"

"She good to us. And, ain't nobody else love her. The

218

white folk hate her for teaching us. And she ain't allowed to live near the colored folk and . . ."

"Why can't she live near you?"

"The law. Whites go one way—coloreds go another."

Maybe that's why we live outside town proper—maybe the Jim Crow laws don't allow Sicilians to live anywhere inside town, not with the whites, not with the Negroes.

Patricia's still talking. "And since our parents never get to know Miss Clarrie, they never get over being afeared of her. You know, feeling stupid around her."

"Oh." I sigh. Miss Clarrie's got it worse than Sicilians; there's only one of her. "She must be lonely."

"So you got to love your teacher. Rest now, Calogero." She closes her eyes.

I stare up at a spiderweb. Then I move a little closer to Patricia.

"Don't go getting no ideas. Move away, Calogero. Now. Scat."

One kiss. What would one kiss hurt? I close my eyes. And I'm inside that first kiss we had, out in the dark of night. The taste of her. I open my eyes. I can't let myself think of the second kiss, behind the rose trellis, or I'll never sleep.

Something's moving down under this loft. *Pad pad pad.* My whole body clutches. A panther? I shimmy silently on my stomach to the edge and peek down. An animal walks up the wall. Rings on its tail. A raccoon.

"Hey," I call. "Scat!"

That raccoon turns and runs headfirst down the wall and disappears. I never saw something that big run downwards headfirst before.

I'll stand guard. Except I've got no weapon if something big comes.

I climb down from the loft, which turns out to be harder than climbing up, and search around. The only thing I find is a heavy glass tube with a bulge at one end. I stick it inside my shirt and climb up into the loft again. And I wait.

The rain stops. Late sunlight slowly comes in through the gable opening. Sweat rolls from my temples down my neck. The air grows even stuffier than it was before.

Patricia sleeps on.

Somewhere far off a bell rings. Daylight is long in July. I crawl to the edge of the gable opening and take the glass tube out of my shirt. It's red. I hold it up to the sun.

"Glory, what a light." Patricia crawls over beside me.

I smile at her. "Sleepyhead."

"A conductor's lantern. From the trains. Where'd you find it?"

"Down below." I hand it to her.

She holds it up and the light streams through onto her cheeks. "Imagine being on a train. Going someplace. Like Miss Clarrie say we should do."

"I'll take you places. We'll see the world together."

She smiles. "Where you going to take me?"

"New Orleans. And that's only the first place."

"Some dream." Her smile stays. "This glass sure beautiful."

"It's yours," I say. "But I'll carry it home for you."

"A gift, huh? A dream and a gift. Reckon that'll buy you a kiss?"

"Ain't got no idea what'll buy me a kiss."

"Now you acting smart, Calogero. Finally. A kiss got to be given." She sets down the lantern glass and puts her hands lightly on my cheeks.

I touch the center of her back at the waist. Just a hint. She moves to me, natural as water running downhill.

twenty-two

Frank Raymond shakes his head. "I already told you. Don't lay that paint on so thick." His voice is sharp.

"It's hard."

"It wouldn't be if you'd take your time."

My fingers tighten around the brush. I'm not getting any better; I'm sick of these painting lessons. "You're yelling."

"You're being clumsy."

I slam the brush down on the table. "I quit." Then I turn to him. "Why are you so ornery today?"

"Ornery? Who taught you that word? That's a Louisiana word. Listen to your drawl. Next thing I know, all my teaching's going to be lost."

I stare at him. "This isn't a good day for me, either. I'm going home."

"Go ahead. All you are is trouble, anyway," yells Frank Raymond.

"Me? What did I do?"

"You and your uncle. I'm back to eating my own lousy grub. Because of you."

"What are you talking about?"

"John Wilson. He finally found out. Your uncle sold that cursèd lemon liquor for the Fourth of July and drove the man nuts. He knows I tutor you. See? Get it now?"

"He won't allow you in the saloon."

"You really are a genius, Calogero." He snorts. "I got used to eating better when I was working there, and Wilson liked the mural so much, he said I could eat half price from then on. But now the whole arrangement's ruined."

"Eat with us. Carlo loves company. You can have *limoncello*. Come tonight."

He puts his flat palm over his mouth and slowly wipes down his chin. "All right."

"Good."

"So." He takes a deep breath and slaps his palm on his chest a few times. "So. Now you tell me, why's this not a good day for you?"

"Because of Mr. Coleman."

"What'd he do?"

"It isn't just him. It's Coleman and Wilson and Rogers and all of them. There's a tournament today. Right now, in fact."

"I know. So?" Frank Raymond raises an eyebrow.

"Well, there's a big supper afterward on a steamboat. And I wanted to work in the kitchen with my friends. But Coleman won't hire me. No one will hire me. Coleman told my friend dagoes are worse than trash, 'cause they'll do anything to you."

"Coleman's an idiot."

"He said dagoes will kill you. Americans believe Sicilians are murderers."

"Not all Americans. It's a Louisiana disease."

"No, it's bigger than that. I read it in newspapers from all over the country. From Washington state to Massachusetts to New York."

"So much for the intelligence of our news reporting." Frank Raymond runs his hands through his hair. "Tell me, how bad do you need the money?"

"It isn't just the money. I wanted to see the inside of a steamboat."

Frank Raymond smiles. "Clean up these paints, Calogero. We're going out."

I open my mouth to ask more, and he shushes me.

We place the paint jars in their boxes and wash the

brushes. Then Frank Raymond puts on fancy clothes. He looks me up and down. "Those your best clothes?"

It's Sunday, of course. And Father May's in town. He's staying all week for some reason. He gave a service this morning, so I dressed right. "Yes."

"That will have to do, then. Stay by me. A tournament in a county seat, well, not much beats that. That's stop number one."

We walk to the courthouse. People were just arriving when I passed earlier, but I never guessed so many would have come in the meantime. They sit perched on surreys and buggies parked in the street. Some have added elevated benches for a better view.

And there's Francesco with Carlo beside him on our wagon bench. Standing in the wagon bed are Rosario and Giuseppe. I can't spy Cirone.

We snake through to the edge of the wide, wide lawn, with me keeping to the far side of Frank Raymond, out of Francesco's line of sight—if he sees me, he'll make me stay with him. Two small boys jostle us as they run by with popguns. Women in gowns, all pleated and puffy, sit on chairs. Men in evening coats, even in this heat, stand behind them with white kid gloves on. White silk handkerchiefs peek from their breast pockets.

Frank Raymond sees me gawking and he pulls a red cotton handkerchief from his hip pocket. He folds it neatly and tucks it at the neck of my shirt. I pat it and I'm happy.

"What in hell do you think you're doing?" comes a harsh voice.

Frank Raymond and I look at a whiskered man wearing spectacles.

"This area's for whites. Get out of here, boy." He looks at Frank Raymond. "Red handkerchief on a dago. You must be plum crazy. If it wasn't such a happy day for the town, I'd make sure y'all got fined. This ain't some cockamamie New York."

"I'm from Iowa." Frank Raymond's voice has a small, angry tremble. "Straight north up the Mississippi from here." He draws a map in the air.

"I know where Iowa's at. What are you—eighteen, nineteen? You're just an overgrown boy who ain't nearly as smart as he thinks. Let me help you out with a lesson, son: insolence ain't the proper attitude for someone far from home." The man walks on.

Then he stops and comes back. "Everyone's got an eye out for the first sign of trouble." He glares at me. "Ain't no one going to disturb the peace of our Tallulah. Y'all going to learn that. One way or another."

"It doesn't matter," I say softly. "I'd rather stand in the side street." I leave.

Frank Raymond follows me out to the road. We stop beside a small group of boys having a yo-yo contest. I look around. A brass band plays on the courthouse steps. All the musicians are Negro, wearing white clothes. The ladies on the chairs and the gentlemen standing behind them are white. But the crowd beyond them, spilling into the street, surrounding the buggies, that's all Negroes. Except for my uncles' wagon.

Frank Raymond rubs his neck again. "That was Mr. Snyder."

"The one that runs the *Madison Journal*?"

"How'd you know that?"

"His name's on it. I must have read it a hundred times at your place."

"Well, good," says Frank Raymond. "You paid attention. He's worth watching out for. All the bigwigs are. Especially the school board."

"Will I meet them when I go to public school?"

"Nope. They won't have anything to do with what happens in your school. They're supposed to, but they won't. Your teacher will do as she pleases."

"Good."

Frank Raymond cocks his head and laughs. "A genius, like I said."

An old woman with a checked apron and a white bonnet walks through the crowd selling fresh peach preserves, the first of the summer. A man tosses a clay saucer high and another man shoots at it. Blue fragments shower the large open area on the lawn. A girl gets up from her chair and shoots. Everyone cheers for her. Now men dressed as knights in royal blues and reds ride out from behind the courthouse on black horses, waving plumes. The crowd hoots and cheers as they parade past.

And they're all white—the peach lady, the shooters, the knights, anyone doing anything other than just watching or playing in the band. I'm starting to feel weak-kneed, as if I'll fall; and I don't know if it's the sun or the Jim Crow laws or both.

I look back at the knights. They each hold a lance at rest. A horn blasts. A knight rides up to a lady in the chairs and, very loudly, he announces he's doing this for her. Then he turns and gallops with his lance pointed forward, straight for a tall pole. A scarlet ring hangs from it. He tries to get that ring on his lance. No luck. The next knight goes up to a different lady and declares himself. Then he has a go at it.

Frank Raymond whispers in my ear, "That's called tilting."

But I don't care anymore. I walk down the street.

Frank Raymond catches up. "So you're not taken with this medieval garbage?"

I shrug. Behind us the crowd cheers. I turn and look. The seated audience climbs onto horses or into buggies, and heads toward the river.

"Off to the steamboat," says Frank Raymond. "Let's get your horses."

"They're harnessed to the wagon. See there? We've got to stay out of sight."

He gives a low whistle. "Without horses, we can't go. It's over eighteen miles to Delta, and that's where the steamboat's docked. I'm sorry, Calogero."

I watch the buggies leave, lurching over rocks and stumps in the road. People stand on either side as far as I can see and wave handkerchiefs as they pass.

The inside of my head buzzes. Mr. Snyder's tone, the sneer when he looked at me, left my brain scrambled, as if I don't know which way is up. And there was something familiar about it. I bet one of the bully boys is his son. "It's just as well Francesco has the horses," I manage to say. "They probably wouldn't have allowed me on that steamboat anyway."

Frank Raymond's face is all blotchy, angry and sad. "Shut your eyes."

"Why?"

"Just do it."

I squeeze my eyes shut.

"Walk up a plank. Lots of people. Women in those dresses—you know, chiffon and silk and whatever. High ceilings with glass chandeliers. People dancing the polka to violins. A gambling casino, with men already moaning over losses. A dining area with raw oysters in tubs of ice and berries in silver bowls. And ham with crackers; caviar and salted salmon and sardines. Bowls of canned peaches floating in syrup."

"It sounds like a palace."

"The sleeping quarters are small, but the drawers are velvet lined and the mirrors are beveled." Frank Raymond stops talking.

I don't know what *beveled* means, but it doesn't matter. I open my eyes. "Thank you."

He walks now, and we slowly go west, the opposite way from the procession. "After the war steamers carried people and cargo along the river all the time. Then they rebuilt the railroads in 1870 and put most of the steamers out of business. Today they're used for traveling circuses or gambling or theatrical shows. Or parties, like this one."

"It would be fun to see a circus," I say, trying to keep my voice normal, like him.

"A circus boat is coming in autumn. A sign in Blander's barbershop says there'll be elephants and ring performers. It'll take days just to disembark and set up the show."

"When in autumn?"

"After the cotton finishes. When everyone's got money to lose. And they will. Tell you one thing I saw. When I was ten years old, my dad took me traveling along the river in late October. We were actually near here, and there was a fire on a steamer."

"You saw a fire?"

"The boilers exploded and the entire boat was consumed."

"Was anyone hurt?"

"I don't think so. My dad bought us two horses and we left fast. It spooked him."

I look at Frank Raymond in wonder. He's only four years older than me, but he always seems to know everything. "How did you learn so much?"

We're already at the far edge of town. He turns up West Street. "I don't know anything compared to what there is to know. But what managed to get into my head is there through two things: travel and study. I read everything my father put in front of me till he died. Then I joined the seminary and . . ."

"The seminary? So why aren't you a preacher?"

"I thought about the things God lets happen, and decided I didn't want to be His voice on earth. So I left after only a year. I painted my way down the Mississippi, staying with rich people while I did family portraits—and they had libraries that I lost myself in for days." Frank Raymond crosses the road to a blackberry thicket. He drops berries in my palm. "The Mississippi is just the start. There's a whole world out there, Calogero. Travel. Don't let men like Snyder define how you see things. He wears blinders, like a horse." His voice breaks. He presses his lips together. "Don't let them put blinders on you: travel."

First, Miss Clarrie and now, Frank Raymond. Maybe travel is the religion of all teachers.

We pick berries till the mosquitoes come on fierce. We slap like crazy. "You ever gambled on one of the steamers?" I ask.

"Never had anything to gamble with." He looks at me

sideways. "But I've watched. Once, I saw a man lose a whole plantation."

"Really? He must have wanted to shoot himself."

"No. He shot the man who won."

I stare. "He killed him?"

"No, but he went to jail for shooting him." He chews on his bottom lip.

And I notice now—his face really does look thinner than it did last week.

"All that imaginary food you painted in my head was good. But I'm wondering, you hungry for real food yet?"

"Ha!"

"Let's go home."

twenty-three

Bang bang bang!

Cirone and I jump up and out of bed. We stand in the hot, dark night turning in circles, stupid as chickens.

Bang bang bang!

"Who's there?" calls Carlo in Sicilian.

"Who?" shouts Francesco in English.

"Open this damn door before I bust it down."

"Dr. Hodge? That you?" Francesco goes to the door.

Rosario lights a candle and we all follow Francesco.

Francesco opens the door and Bedda comes skittering in.

"Goats! You and your cursèd goats! There were three of them on my porch tonight. Three! How many times do I have to tell you? You keep your goats at home or I'll shoot them. This is the last warning. You hear me?"

"You shout. Everybody hear you. God, He hear you."

"It's Tuesday, God's working day, my working day, your working day. So He better hear. And you better hear. Tie up those infernal goats!" Dr. Hodge stumbles off the edge of the porch. He brushes at his cloak and disappears into the night.

Francesco closes the door. "Get back to bed," he says to us all in Sicilian.

We stand here.

"Bedda's still inside," I say at last.

"She can stay inside. Tomorrow after supper you tie her back legs together. That way she won't go wandering."

Carlo makes the sign of the cross, then he looks upward with gratitude on his face. That's how I feel, too.

"What about the other two?" says Rosario. "Dr. Hodge said there were three."

"The others are idiots. They follow Bedda. She doesn't go, they don't go. Get back to sleep."

Rosario blows out the candle.

I fall onto the bed and roll on my side, away from Cirone's feet.

Bedda jumps onto Francesco's bed. He pushes her off. She clomps around the room, around and around. Finally, she makes a loud snort and drops *clunk* on the floor beside Francesco's bed. She groans. Francesco sits up and looks at her. "Oh, damn. All right." Bedda jumps onto his bed and settles down. "Nobody's going to shoot you," murmurs Francesco. "Dr. Hodge was just angry. Nobody shoots goats. Goats are too important. And Dr. Hodge is a decent man. He wouldn't do that to me; he likes me. But from now on, you stay here at night. Understand?"

The room goes quiet.

After a while a whisper comes: "Calo."

I roll to face Cirone.

"You think Hodge had on his nightdress under that cloak?" He's speaking English. That's all he ever uses with me these days.

"I don't know," I whisper back. "But it sure must be hot under there in this weather. Hot enough to make me glad I'm no gentleman and I don't wear cloaks."

"Maybe he ain't got nothing on at all under it." Cirone laughs softly. "He looked like a big loggerhead, he was so angry."

"Like the one that mashed your foot?"

"Nah, that one was little. He looked like a giant snapper."

I gulp. "Have you seen a giant snapper?"

Cirone doesn't answer.

I push myself up on my elbows. "Tell me."

"Stay down or you're going to get us both in trouble."

"Did you go back to Alligator Bayou? Did you go with the boys without me?"

"Loggerheads sell for a dollar fifty apiece. A giant one sells for two dollars."

Where was I? Where was I when Cirone was out hunting turtles? "How much did you make?"

"Five dollars. But split among the four of us."

"Still, a lot."

"Don't be jealous. You hate the swamp."

That's not the point. "What else have you done without me?"

"It don't matter."

"It does too. I met them first."

"So?"

"So they're my friends first."

"That ain't how it works and you know it. Friends is like teeth; ignore them and they go away."

"Who taught you to say that?"

"Ben's mamma."

Cirone's been in Ben's house. I want to punch something. "I haven't acted unfriendly."

"Come on, Calo. Who'd you spend time with at the Fourth of July picnic?"

Patricia. If I have to choose between the boys and Patricia, she's my choice. But I don't want to choose. "Can we all do something together? Maybe tomorrow night?"

"Tomorrow?" says Cirone. "I'll ask the others."

"Thanks."

Wednesday supper is like a party. Frank Raymond is here, but that's no surprise. When he showed up with me on Sunday and raved about the spaghetti, Carlo insisted he come back every night. The first tomatoes from our own garden were in the sauce that night—so good.

Tonight Father May is here, too. That makes it a party. It turns out Frank Raymond knows a lot about the Catholic religion, though he's Lutheran. And Father May likes to drink wine, whether it's part of the Mass or not. Supper so far has been a long discussion about popes and the method for choosing the next one. Pope Leo XIII is almost ninety years old, after all.

My uncles don't talk. Probably they stopped listening, since the conversation is fast and in English. Cirone and I don't talk, either. Cirone keeps yawning. I have to work to keep my own mouth shut.

Frank Raymond turns to Cirone. "What do you think of all this?"

"I don't," says Cirone.

That was rude. I kick him under the table.

"What about you, Calogero?"

"The cardinals will do a good job choosing someone else."

"How can you be so sure?"

"They always do."

"Hmm." Frank Raymond looks at Father May. "If the

cardinals always did a good job choosing a new pope, do you think that would constitute a miracle?" He laughs.

Father May doesn't laugh. "The nature of a miracle is no joke."

Frank Raymond's face goes serious. "What is a miracle, Father?"

My uncles come to attention. The English word *miracle*—so close to our word *miraculu*—is dear to them.

"A wonder. A power given to a human by God, to show His grace."

"Is having a baby a miracle?" asks Cirone.

I blink at him. "What a dumb question. A mouse can have a baby."

"You really think it's dumb?" Frank Raymond folds his arms on the table and leans toward me. "It's life where there wasn't life before."

"Calogero's right," says Father May. "A mouse can do it. A cockroach can do it. It's natural. A miracle isn't natural. It must be divine. It must be something that happens only through the grace of God."

"Dead." Carlo speaks slowly and deliberately. I know it's because he feels odd saying an English word, but the effect is that it feels like a pronouncement from on high. We all look at him. "Dead . . . then alive."

"Right," says Father May. "Raising the dead is a miracle."

"Water, wine," says Giuseppe. This may be the first time I've ever heard him speak English.

"Turning water into wine," says Father May. "That's right. That's a miracle."

"Hmm," says Frank Raymond. "That makes me think of what Spinoza said. He called miracles violations of nature."

Father May stands, his mouth open in shock. "Spinoza was a Jew."

"So?"

Father May looks from Frank Raymond to me. "Has he been teaching you heretical ideas?"

"He's a good teacher. We don't talk about God."

"A good teacher who does not talk about God?" Father May's voice rises. "That's impossible—a contradiction."

Francesco clears his throat and puts up his hand: halt. "The English, it go too fast." He turns to me. "What's happening?" he asks in Sicilian.

"They're fighting about miracles and what some Jew said."

"Quick," Francesco says to Giuseppe in Sicilian, "get out the *grappa*. And, Carlo, didn't you make a sweet tonight?"

"I made pie from those orange potatoes." He used the English word *pie* in the middle of his Sicilian sentence. Now he looks at me, a little shyly. "Are you happy, Calogero? Giuseppe told me that's what you wanted."

"Sure I'm happy." But I wonder where Carlo got a recipe.

Giuseppe is already pouring Frank Raymond a small glass of *grappa*. Now he pours one for Father May.

Frank Raymond lifts his glass to us, then downs it all at once. He falls off the bench coughing. No one drinks a glass of *grappa* in one big gulp. It's like fire blasting through your chest, exploding your stomach.

Francesco pats him hard on the back and offers water.

Frank Raymond's eyes stream and he coughs and coughs. Then he stands up straight. "What was that?"

"Grappa," I say. "You're supposed to sip it."

"Like this." Father May sits and takes a small sip. "My compliments to the maker."

Frank Raymond looks at Father May. Then he laughs.

Father May's mouth twitches. Then he laughs, too. And we're all laughing.

Carlo brings in the sweet potato pie. But it's not pie at all. It's a layer of dough with thinly sliced sweet potato arranged in overlapping rows. It's nothing like Patricia's recipe, or anyone else's, I bet. "So, Calogero," he says in Sicilian, "what do you think?" He proudly thrusts his face forward over the baking tray.

"It'll be perfect with *grappa*."

Frank Raymond grabs the bottle from the table and pours me a little. I spoke in Sicilian—but Frank Raymond must have picked out the word *grappa*. I dip in my tongue tip and savor the burn.

We eat the dessert. It's far from delicious.

Carlo frowns. "Sicilian sweets are better."

We move to the front porch and the men smoke cigars and drink more *grappa*. In little sips. Frank Raymond refills my glass.

"Don't get drunk," Cirone says in my ear. "We're sneaking out tonight."

The conversation is a mix of Sicilian, English, and French, with Latin speckled here and there. I don't believe anyone is listening to anyone else anymore. Finally, Father May and Frank Raymond leave together. The rest of us go to bed.

"Come on." Cirone pinches my cheeks.

My eyes opened at his words, but it took the pinches to pull me together. I run my tongue along the top of my mouth, scraping it against my front teeth. The *grappa* left a cottony feeling. I roll out of bed and pull on clothes and follow Cirone outside.

We lope through the grasses toward town. It's drizzling lightly. I tilt my head back and open my mouth. This feels good. "Where are we going?"

"Speak English," says Cirone in English.

"You heard me," I say in English.

"The courthouse. Your favorite spot." We run in easy strides.

Only one boy stands on the sidewalk waiting. "You

always last, you know that?" It's Rock. He spits on the ground in annoyance.

"We had guests," says Cirone. "They didn't leave till late."

"But we're not last, anyway," I say. "Ben and Charles aren't here yet."

"They came and went. We got work in the morning, and Mr. Coleman extra mean for some reason. We got to be there at six o'clock on the dot. I only stayed so you wouldn't get here and act dumb, walking in circles shouting for us. Good night."

"We got work in the morning, too," says Cirone.

"Then go sleep." Rock waves and turns to leave.

Bang! Bang bang bang.

"Guns," gasps Rock. "Run!"

We're already gone.

twenty-four

I'm out of the house before breakfast, calling, "Bedda! Bedda!" Where is that goat? The little doe Giada runs to me. So do Carina and Furba, and the young billy Duci, and all the others. But Bedda's nowhere in sight. Neither is Bruttu, the old billy. My stomach turns. Please, don't let this be so. I run toward the field. "Bedda! Bedda!"

"Come back, Calo." Cirone grabs me by the elbow.

"I didn't tie her back legs."

Cirone chews the corner of his thumb. "I forgot, too." He's speaking Sicilian. Somehow that makes things seem more real. But it can't be. It has to be a nightmare.

243

Don't, Lord, please please don't.

Everyone's at the breakfast table when we come in. We eat in silence.

"So, Calogero." Francesco puts down his coffee cup and stands. "You were out there calling a goat. A goat who didn't come."

He loves that goat. I can't stand it that I did this to him. "I'm sorry, Francesco. I forgot. I'm so sorry."

"I forgot, too," Cirone says.

Francesco's mouth is a straight line. But now it quivers at one edge. Why does it have to be Bedda? Of all the goats, why her? He clears his throat and pulls on the tips of his mustache. "Let's go find out if it's too late for sorry. You and me, Calo. It was your job."

I walk with Francesco into town. We go straight to Dr. Hodge's office. Bedda and Bruttu lie on the porch. Flies cover them.

Dr. Hodge comes out immediately. He must have been watching from the window. His hands are behind his back.

Francesco doesn't look at him. His eyes are on the bodies. "You shoot my goat."

"I warned you."

"You shoot my goat." Francesco shakes his head slowly, like it weighs so much he can hardly hold it up. Tears stand in his eyes. "You shoot my goat. My heart, it go like this." He snaps his fingers. Then he drops his hand. "Now you better shoot me."

I can't believe he said that.

Dr. Hodge's eyes open larger. "Don't be absurd. I was afraid you'd come at me with your stiletto. But crying. Don't do that. You're a businessman. Act like one. Be sensible."

"You shoot my goat," Francesco says so quietly I'm almost not sure he spoke. He puts his hand over his heart. "Now you better shoot me."

"You people, you're all crazy. But, so help me God, I'll shoot you if I have to."

We walk to the grocery on leaden feet, go in through the rear door. Francesco sits on the iron bed in the storage room, his hands in his lap.

The bed is piled high with empty crates. I would move some aside, to sit near Francesco, but I don't know if he wants me there.

I stand in front of him. "I'm sorry." I have to stop talking or I'll cry.

We stay that way a long time. The air grows hotter and stuffier. We pant.

Someone knocks on the front door.

"Should I open the store?"

"We're not open today. Today we're in mourning."

"I'll go out front and tell people."

Francesco doesn't answer.

I go around to stand on the front step. When people come, I tell them we're closed for *luttu*—I don't know the

English word for mourning. I know so many words. Reading the newspaper has taught me thousands and thousands. But that one is missing.

People don't seem to mind, though. They don't ask what *luttu* is. They just go away. Maybe they think it's some crazy Sicilian ritual. Maybe they all think we're crazy. Maybe it's not just Dr. Hodge.

Crazy murderers. Dr. Hodge said he thought Francesco would come after him with a stiletto. And he's an educated man. Like Mr. Snyder. All these educated men. But Dr. Hodge—how could he? He knows us.

I sit on the front step now. As the morning passes, I realize: no one white has come by. They all know the store is closed. They know what's happened. It's like they're one giant family, news passes among them so fast.

Carlo brings food at midday. He tries to get Francesco to come home with him. Francesco stays put on the bed.

I sit on the front step all afternoon. How could I have forgotten to tie Bedda's legs? I love Francesco. I hate myself for doing this to him. I rest my arms on my knees and my head on my arms and I sleep.

Evening comes. Rosario and Cirone show up. We walk around to the back of the grocery and go in to see Francesco.

"I closed the stand early," says Rosario. "Let's go home now. It's time to eat."

Francesco actually gets up. Thank heavens.

We walk home and Carlo serves spaghetti with tomatoes and homemade venison sausage. Francesco's favorite meal. No one speaks as we eat.

"It was good." I wipe my bowl clean with a hunk of bread. "Thank you, Carlo."

"I'll go sit on the grocery step now," says Carlo. "You go to bed, Francesco."

"It's still light out."

"Sorrow doesn't care about the light. Go to bed." Carlo presses his palm to his forehead. "I'm off to the grocery."

"I'll go with you," says Giuseppe.

"Why?" I ask. "No one will come shopping at night."

"Let them go," says Francesco. "It's better that they should sit there. It's better that everyone should know we're in mourning."

"Everyone knows already," I say.

"But they have to hear our side," says Francesco. "They have to know that Dr. Hodge killed our goats. He was supposed to like us. To respect us."

"Carlo and Giuseppe can't tell them our side. They don't speak English."

"Then you go with them. You be the translator." Francesco hangs his head that sad way again and shakes it. "He called us 'you people.' He said we're crazy. Dr. Hodge, he said those things. He shot our goats, and he said those things."

Carlo and Giuseppe and I go back to the grocery. They

sit on the step and I walk back and forth on the sidewalk out front. The first stars show through the dusk.

A clattering noise comes from inside the grocery.

"Rats," says Giuseppe. "I'll take care of them." He goes around the rear. I hear him walking inside. He opens the front door and looks out at us.

"You!" shouts Carlo in English from beside me.

I whirl around and look where he's pointing.

Dr. Hodge is walking along the sidewalk with the man who runs the candy store, Mr. Chehardy. Dr. Hodge looks at Carlo, stops, and stands at attention.

"You broke my little brother's heart," Carlo says in Sicilian.

"Don't speak that mumbo jumbo at me," says Dr. Hodge.

"You made him think you were his friend," Carlo says in Sicilian as he walks toward Dr. Hodge. "You fooled him. But you never fooled me. You broke my baby brother's heart."

"No one understands you, old man. No one understands any of you. Get out of my way." Dr. Hodge walks on.

Carlo lunges at him.

"Don't stab!" yelps Dr. Hodge. He beats Carlo on the head with one fist and pulls out a pistol.

Lord! What's going on? "Stop!" I shout. "Carlo doesn't have a knife. He doesn't have anything."

Dr. Hodge has the pistol in both hands now and he's using it like a club, smashing Carlo in the forehead. Smashing and smashing, as if he's lost his mind. Blood gushes.

I run to grab Dr. Hodge from behind.

"Get out of the way, Calogero!" Giuseppe's standing in the doorway with a double-barreled shotgun!

Where are you, Lord?

"Look out, Doctor!" calls someone across the street.

Arms grab me from behind. I stumble backward.

"Be quiet," he says in my ear. It's Joe Evans. "Run home. Get Francesco." He lets me go and races off down the first street.

Dr. Hodge shoots at Giuseppe and misses. He slams the pistol even harder on Carlo's head. Carlo crumples.

"Stay down," Giuseppe calls to Carlo. "Stay out of the way so I can shoot."

Dr. Hodge backs into the middle of the road and aims at Giuseppe again. He presses his finger over and over, but his gun won't shoot. He must have broken it on Carlo's head. He pulls his cloak closed to hide himself.

Giuseppe aims—*bang bang.*

Dr. Hodge still stands. Blood runs down his leg. "Someone give me a gun!"

Giuseppe jumps off the step and picks up Carlo. Together we carry him inside the grocery and lay him on the floor. "Go for Francesco," Giuseppe says.

I run home. "Giuseppe shot Dr. Hodge!"

Francesco jumps off his bed, still fully dressed. "Is he dead?"

"No."

"Did he shoot back?"

"He shot first, and missed. When he tried again, his gun wouldn't work. He broke it on Carlo's head."

Francesco's already got his cap on and he's halfway out the door with Rosario and Cirone right behind. "Where are they?"

"At the grocery."

"We'll go to Carlo and Giuseppe. But you, Calogero . . ." Francesco squeezes my arm. "You go find Father May."

Francesco and Rosario and Cirone and me, we all go running back toward town.

And there's Dr. Hodge limping down the street toward his office with a crowd of people in tow.

"Go for Father May," Francesco shouts to me.

I turn a corner and run.

But I hear the crowd. They surround Francesco and Rosario and Cirone.

I run flat out. Father May is staying in the guesthouse on the other side of town. It's so far. We need help faster than that.

Frank Raymond.

I turn up the next street. There's a crowd outside Wilson's saloon, directly across from Blander's barbershop. I press myself against the wall and pray the shadows hide me as I make my way toward Frank Raymond's.

"Bloodthirsty things!" shouts John Wilson. "They stayed in that grocery all day. What do you think they was doing? Plotting. They was plotting this murder."

Murder? What murder?

"Our good doctor. Our dear doctor!"

He's crazy! Dr. Hodge is alive!

"Y'all heard them bragging, didn't you? They said they already killed two white clerks at a plantation store and they could do as they pleased because they got the money to get out of anything. Did you notice that? Did you notice how they always takes your money, but they never spends theirs? They got so much, they make the rest of us look like paupers."

What's he talking about? How could my uncles brag? They don't even speak English. When would any of us ever even go into a plantation store?

"Sicilians, they's the worst." It's Mr. Rogers, Willy's father. "More monkeys than people. I hear they shot the good doctor in the groin. That's how low they stoop."

"Cold-blooded murderers." It's Mr. Coleman. "They killed our doctor and he's our coroner, too. How we going to get along without him?"

"Y'all cross them and they never forget," says Mr. Rogers. "They'll murder without a second look."

"We got a scourge on our hands," says John Wilson.

"Tell you what, folks: my saloon is open. Free whisky and beer to any responsible soul who will help wipe out this scourge."

"They already got three of them," comes a cry. It's Fred Johnson. "I saw Sheriff Lucas and his deputies haul them off to jail."

"Jail? Jail's too good for them animals." John Wilson shakes a fist in the air. "Anyway, they ain't got them two did the shooting. As I hear it, they's still back at the grocery. Probably plotting who to kill next."

"I ain't waiting around to see who it'll be." One man raises a rope.

I gag.

Someone steps in front of me and presses his back up against me so hard that I'm squashed against the wall. "Stay quiet!" comes a sharp whisper. It's Frank Raymond.

The crowd goes down the street toward our grocery like a herd of wild things.

Frank Raymond stays there for what feels like forever. Then he turns around and holds me up by the shoulders. "Blander told me you were here. You're crazy."

"What'll they do with that rope?"

"We've got to get you out of here."

"We've got to find Giuseppe and Carlo. We've got to get the others out of jail. We've got to tell the truth. Dr. Hodge is alive. No one killed anyone."

"Shut up."

"They—"

Frank Raymond claps his hand over my mouth. "No one can stop a mob. All you can do is get out of the way. You understand?"

I nod.

He lets go of me. "Let's . . ."

"You find Father May!" I run before he can say more.

I'm running and running, but when I get to the grocery, no one's there. The front door's closed and the back's been bashed in. I go inside. The bed in the storage room is overturned. The chair by the chimney is on its side. There are voices outside. Coming closer. I go into the front room and press myself into a corner and sink to my haunches. If they have a lantern, I'm caught.

A man and boy come into the storage room. "Looks like the show has already moved on to the slaughterhouse, son." They leave.

The slaughterhouse. I'm going to be sick.

Someone else comes in through the rear door. "Calogero? Calogero?" Frank Raymond squats before me.

"The slaughterhouse," I manage to say.

"I know. And there's talk of storming the jail. And of catching other Sicilians, two others, in Milliken's Bend."

"Beppe and Salvatore." I stand up quick. "Someone's got to warn them."

"Father May took care of that. He's friends with someone who knows them. I promise."

I'm crying.

"It's insane." Frank Raymond throws his arms around me and holds tight.

"It's my fault. I forgot to tie up Bedda."

"Stop it. None of this is your fault. And you have to get someplace safe. You have to think of yourself now. Have you got a place to go?"

"Yes."

"Then go. Run away. Don't tell me where. I don't want to know. That way if the mob gets hold of me, I can't tell them anything, no matter what they do."

twenty-five

I run the road out of town, but as soon as Frank Raymond's out of sight, I turn and race back. The shortest way
to the slaughterhouse is to cut through town. I'm slick with
sweat and panting hard and the only noise I hear is my own
heartbeat. I've got to get there fast. I run in the center of the
road. Others are running, too. But not as fast as me.

I can see it now. The slaughterhouse is lit up so bright,
it looks as if it's on fire. Outside, people stand in the grasses
in little clumps of three or four. Whites with whites;
Negroes with Negroes. Everyone's talking. Children race

through the crowd playing tag. More people are coming. The people I ran past on the road, they're coming here.

If anyone recognizes me . . . I race for the woods, expecting to hear a shout, maybe even a shot. I dash behind a pine and cling. The bark cuts my cheek. People are coming in buggies, like to the tournament. Coming for a show, all right.

Sheriff Lucas! Get here fast!

I hunch over, run to the closest window, and press myself against the rear wall. I pull up on the window ledge and look in.

Giuseppe and Carlo are on their knees with their backs to me. Their hands are tied behind them. Men stand in front of them, arguing, everyone talking at once. White men. I can make out faces. John Wilson, Mr. Rogers, Fred Johnson, and others. And, Lord in Heaven, there's Frank Raymond and Mr. Blander.

"All of them did it," says Wilson in a booming voice.

For a second everyone's quiet.

"This ain't no court of law," says Blander in a flat tone. "They's procedures to follow. Facts to gather."

"We done gathered the facts," says Wilson.

"No, you didn't." Frank Raymond steps forward, but Blander catches him by the arm. Frank Raymond shakes him off. "They have a right to defend themselves."

"You want a trial?" Rogers turns to Giuseppe. "Who killed Dr. Hodge?"

"No one!" shouts Frank Raymond. "He's not dead! Dr. Hodge is alive!"

Giuseppe mumbles in Sicilian. I'm not sure he even understands the question.

"And you?" Rogers leans toward Carlo. "What you got to say for yourself?"

If Carlo speaks, I can't hear it. He keeps jerking his right shoulder forward, pulling against the rope on his hands. And I know, I just know, he wants to make the sign of the cross.

"All right." Rogers juts his chin toward Frank Raymond. "They got their trial."

"Hodge isn't dead!" says Frank Raymond. "We've got to wait for Sheriff Lucas."

"No more trouble from y'all, Mr. Raymond," growls Rogers.

"Father May isn't here. They're Catholic. They need a priest."

"Catholics. They swarm all over New Orleans and Baton Rouge, but we keep clean of them here in Tallulah. That priest ain't even American. He's as bad as these dagoes."

A man whose face I can't see points a gun toward Frank Raymond and Blander.

"No more wasting time." Johnson throws a rope over the crossbar where beef carcasses usually hang. The end is tied into a noose. He fits it over Giuseppe's head!

I scream, "No!" But the sound's cut off by a hand over my mouth and I'm rolling on the ground, kicking and biting, and two of them are on me at once.

"Stop it, dumbhead!"

I'm pinned, shaking and staring through the dusk at Rock and Charles.

"Get up." Charles stands and pulls on my arm. "We got to run."

"No."

He drags me toward the woods, but I rip myself away and run for the window again when a cheer comes up from inside the slaughterhouse. Something's happened.

I stop still. The whole world's gone crazy.

"Calogero." The voice is right beside me. "Come on!" Patricia takes my hand.

I don't know what else to do. They pull me along into the woods. Ben is waiting there. We go deeper and I can't hear anything anymore. It's like we're underwater.

I stop in a small clearing, heaving.

"Come on!" Patricia pulls on me. "Hurry."

"I can't go with you."

"You got to."

"I can't."

"Why not?"

"You know why not. You go home now. With Charles. I'm leaving."

She lets out a sob and holds me tight.

I put my hands on her wet cheeks. "I'll come back for you."

She shakes her head.

"I will. I really will. Sooner than you think."

"I ain't never going to forget you, Calogero. Never."

"I'll be back."

"Hurry!" says Ben. "We got to run."

"I'm going alone," I say.

"You ain't got a chance alone in the dark," says Rock.

"I'm going alone!"

Ben grabs my arm and spins me to face him. "All right. Where?"

"I don't know yet."

"Take off your shirt," says Ben.

"What?"

"Hurry."

I take off my shirt.

Ben rips it. He ties half around his ankle and hands the other half to Rock.

Rock ties it around his ankle. "Which way you headed?"

A sudden memory comes of how free I felt that day Frank Raymond and I came out on open water. "The river."

"Direct, or by the road to Delta?"

"Direct."

"I'll run the road," says Rock.

"I'll head to Milliken's Bend," says Ben.

"Are you crazy?"

"Don't worry," says Ben. "We'll fool those hounds with your smelly shirt. But if they get too close, we'll throw away the shirt and climb the closest tree."

"No more talk," says Patricia. She puts her hand in the center of my chest and pushes. "Run. All of you. Calogero, Calogero—run!"

twenty-six

I run through the woods.

Panthers. If you run, they chase.

I have to run. So I should get out of the woods. I come out at the east edge of town and go past houses.

People might see me. A boy running. Suspicious. If a crowd comes after me, the people in these houses could tell what they saw. But I have to run.

My uncles. And Cirone. Oh Lord, Cirone. Cirone! Look what my forgetting did. Lord, save them. Save them. Make a miracle.

Run run run. Tears stream down my face. I can't see anything. But I run. I'm past exhaustion, running as if I could go on forever.

I hear dogs bay. My skin turns to goose flesh. Sheriff Lucas' bloodhounds. They're tracking something. Someone.

Don't let them get Rock or Ben.

I think of the dogs' powerful legs and long muzzles and for an instant I go numb with fear. But I'm still running.

Are the dogs getting louder? They seem louder. And they're coming from only one direction. They didn't split up. They didn't get fooled. I need a plan. But the only thing in my head is the river.

I race. Faster and faster. I stumble and cut my knee and get up and run. The ground gets soft. Now I'm slapping through mud. Cypresses surround me. Lord, I've headed into a swamp!

It's all right. I'll be all right. I slog on, trying to get back to firmer ground. Frank Raymond warned about this swamp. He said it was south of the path we took. So if I head north, I'll find dry land. Only I've lost my bearings. And I can't see the sky, I can't see the stars, the trees are so thick.

A small swamp, he said. Small.

But Patricia said there're 'gators in every swamp. I stifle a scream. There're worse things than 'gators. Patricia said that, too.

The dogs grow loud behind me. I slog on. Mud sucks

at my shoes, slops up my ankles. I look back. Through an opening in the trees I see distant lanterns. The dogs are running ahead of the men. So close.

A shriek. Someone shouts, "Stay back!"

I can't help but look. A 'gator has caught one of the dogs. The 'gator's shaking it and shaking it. The other bloodhound circles at a distance. The lanterns have clustered. The 'gator shakes till the dog's belly rips open.

I'm flying. My feet find dryer ground. I'm running so fast, I'm not even sure I'm breathing.

Will they turn back now? There's still one dog. I run and run till my body is doing it on its own, as though that's all it knows. And I hear the dog bay again.

Something slinks across my path. I stop short, my heart thumping. Another follows it. Otters. Why, I'm already at the river, and the otters are slipping into the water, panic-stricken.

Dogs can't smell through water. And I can swim. I plunge in. I'm only a few feet out when the current catches me, and sweeps me away, down river. I kick like mad just to stay afloat. I hear the dog over the rush of the river. Lanterns bob about in the blackness on shore. Then I'm too far downstream. I can't see anything anymore. The only noise now is the water.

I fight and fight till I'm out of the current and back near shore. A bush branch hangs clear into the water. I catch hold and stay there.

In my head I see Carlo's shoulder jerking; he's trying so hard, so hard, to free his right hand, to make the sign of the cross. It's all I can see; my head has room for nothing else. In the name of the Father, and the Son, and the Holy Ghost.

Starlight glints off the moving water. And I realize the things hanging all around me aren't just leaves; they're closed up damselflies. I fall into a kind of woozy half sleep.

Something screeches behind me on the shore. Then there's a high-pitched *eeeek*.

A woodpecker drums away.

I'm shivering. The air is hot, but somehow my body's losing heat. I don't know how long I've been in the water, but I'm sure at least half the night has passed. I pull myself up by climbing through the bush and I hug the shore as I walk north now. If the dog comes back, the river is close.

North is where Joseph is. Joseph. I'll find Joseph if I just keep walking. Or he'll find me. He could shoot an arrow at me again. Or that musket.

Don't think like that.

I sing inside my head. I sing in Sicilian.

I'm running again. Tiny creatures scatter and bigger ones scurry and I have no idea how far there is left to go. It's barely dawn, so I can't see well enough to recognize landmarks and I'm too crazy anyway and I'm crying again and I'm running.

"Pssst."

I stop.

"Come, friend."

"Joseph." I practically fall against him. "Joseph. Help."

"The Tunica tribe helps orphans."

The word pierces. I wince. "I have to tell you something."

"Come sleep."

"You have to understand. I think they're chasing me."

"I heard the baying. They went away."

"They could come back. Maybe someone saw me. Maybe you'll be in danger, too."

"Come sleep."

"Joseph. They're like the boys who buried you with stones."

"Do you think I am afraid? You are wrong. Come, friend. Talk after you sleep."

We go to his shack and lie down on the earth. I close my eyes. I can't stop crying. "Joseph?" I whisper.

"I am here, friend."

"I have to . . . figure out what to do."

"You will."

"No time. They'll come after me."

"Did you do something bad?"

"I'm Sicilian."

"That."

"My cousin. My uncles." My words crack. Please, Lord,

please let me still have a cousin, uncles. My head throbs as if it would split. "I have to get my . . . tribe."

"The Tunica tribe is the friend of the Sicilian tribe."

"I have to . . . I have to take them away from here. How far is New York?"

"New York is a terrible place."

"What do you know?"

"I cross the river to Vicksburg. I go once a month. I read the newspaper."

"New York . . . We could work making tunnels. Underground railway."

"Do you know what a slum is?"

"No."

"It is where you would live. It is dirty. It is full of disease. And Theodore Roosevelt is the governor. He wants to get rid of Italian slums. He wants to empty them. He does not like Italians."

"Does anyone in America?"

"The Tunica tribe does."

"We need work. How long would it take us to get to New York?"

"With much luck it could take weeks."

"Too far."

"Too far from what?"

"A girl."

"A girl. Does she own a bowl with crisscrosses?"

"Yes. I know how to sell greens. We all do." We. My

family. Please, Lord, please. I roll my head side to side. Please. I push myself up on my elbows. "Wait. A whole town of Sicilians. Tangipahoa Parish. Strawberry farmers."

"A big tribe. That is a good plan. Sleep now."

I lie back and close my eyes. Cirone. Lord, please. A miracle.

I sleep like the dead.

When I open my eyes, Joseph is gone. The air presses on my chest. The shack is an oven.

I am alone.

Am I? Am I really?

The shakes start in my arms. My chest. My teeth chatter. I squeeze my hands together and try to clench my jaw, but I can't. I can't stop the shakes.

Maybe they got away. Just one small miracle, Lord— can't You give me one?

I crawl out. It's past midday. Joseph is nowhere in sight. I drink from the little pond. The water is clean, but it makes me retch. I stuff my fist in my mouth to keep from screaming, and I wait.

Joseph appears silently from the direction of the river. He carries a sack. He sits beside me and hands me a peach.

"I'm not hungry."

"Eat. You need it."

I take a bite. The juice fills my mouth. I'm crying, but I eat. And Joseph eats. We eat peaches and peaches.

I finally stop and wipe my chin. "Where did you get these?"

"I went to Milliken's Bend."

"So far?"

"It is close if you go through the woods. I got provisions for your trip. Everyone talks." He speaks slowly. His eyes fasten on mine. "They are dead."

My lips go tingly. My eyes feel like they will fall from my head. "All of them?"

"All five are dead."

I hug my knees to my chest, but it doesn't stop the shaking. I'm shaking all over, so hard I hear my bones. Cirone. My uncles and cousin—they're dead. The people I love—they're dead. Joseph holds me. I moan into the hollow under his collarbone. I want to climb inside there. I want to disappear.

All five, dead. Five. Slowly the number means something. I pull myself away. I'm not shaking anymore; I'm limp. I whisper, "The two in Milliken's Bend—alive?"

"Buck Collins took them to Vicksburg. He has a skiff."

"Buck Collins?"

"A human being. No one knows about it. Buck will not tell."

"He told you."

"Telling me is not telling."

I lick my bottom lip. "I am alone."

"You are free to become anything."

"No! No! I don't know anymore. I don't know anything."

"That is not true. Let yourself know."

"I didn't tie up Bedda, I know that. Francesco's goat. It mattered, what I didn't do, it mattered."

"To you."

I stare at him.

"You were there. You know what happened. Tell me."

"Goats don't explain what didn't matter. It didn't matter that Carlo never owned a stiletto. It didn't matter that Dr. Hodge shot first. And that he didn't die." I'm crying again. My chest heaves. "They were waiting. Waiting for their chance."

Joseph holds me again.

"Cirone," I sob. "Cirone was thirteen. All he wanted was to be American. He was thirteen. Joseph, he was thirteen. He was . . . he was . . ."

Joseph rocks me. "But there is good, too. Try to think of that. Can you think?"

There's Patricia. Rock. Charles. Ben.

"Think," Joseph says.

There's Frank Raymond. Joe Evans. Mr. Blander. Miss Clarrie.

There's Joseph.

Rocco! My brother, my brother. I pull away and look at Joseph.

He tilts his head. "Do you want more peaches?"

"No."

"Come." Joseph picks up the sack and I follow him through the woods to the river. He puts down the sack and pulls a giant log out from under thick bushes. How can he be that strong? But the log is hollowed out. It's a dugout boat from a cypress log. A long paddle lies in the bottom.

Joseph sets the sack in the boat. "Food. Make it last." He takes a wide hide pouch from around his neck and puts it around mine. "Coins. One dollar." He pats the pouch. "Do not lose it. Also a pipestone bowl. Tunica. People in cities buy pipestone bowls. They think our work is quaint. They will pay high. Make them pay high."

"Cities? Where am I going?"

"When you see a settlement, lie flat. People will see only a log. The river will take you to Baton Rouge. Sell the bowl. Then walk east to Tangipahoa."

"The Mississippi goes straight to Baton Rouge?"

"The great river, the *titik,* does nothing straight. It twists and turns. A sandbar can flip you. A rough patch or sawyer can wreck you."

I shake my head. "I can't do this. Tangipahoa Parish. I can't get there on my own." My body shakes; I walk in a circle. "What's going on? This can't be! I can't–I can't." I lean forward with my hands on my knees.

Joseph grabs me by the arms and his fingers are strong. "You are free. You can choose. You can become what you choose."

He chose to become Joseph.

I stare at the boat. I want to scream. But I hear myself say, "Teach me how to use this."

"The *titik* teaches you. Go to shore at bad spots. *Huri* is light. You can carry it."

"*Huri?*"

"It means 'wind.' It is the name of this boat."

"How long will it take me?"

"In high water I used to do it in five days. But now is the middle of summer. The water is slow. I will push *Huri* into the water. You get in. Move soft, but quick. The current will wash you away." He pushes the boat through the undergrowth.

I can't do this. "Wait. Wait. How will I return *Huri* to you?"

"You will not."

"But how will you go where you want?"

"I do not travel the *titik* anymore."

"You go over to Vicksburg."

"Buck Collins can take me."

He has all the answers.

I can't stall any longer. Men could come looking—any moment. "Joseph, how can I repay you?"

"By letting me help you."

"Thank you, Joseph." I don't want to get in the boat, I don't want to leave Joseph.

We look at each other.

Huri is in the water. And now I am in *Huri.* Joseph pulls, then steps to the side and lets go. The current takes me. I wave goodbye.

Then I face forward. The banks slip by.

My cousin and uncles are gone.

But Rocco waits for me. We're family.

I hear Patricia in my head: "Every human being got his race to run."

I'm running. But I'll be back. Someday.

I will be back.

AFTERWORD

Several years ago I came across an old and brief newspaper article about five Sicilian grocers in Tallulah, Louisiana, in 1899, who served a black customer before a white one because he had entered the store first; they wound up dead–lynched. I was shocked. Bigotry pings the brain into numbness, it seems so inexplicable. But as I dug into the history around the lynching, I found answers that went far beyond bigotry. And numbness gave way to such a searing pain that I had to write this story.

I built characters for this book around people who testified or were talked about in the testaments taken after the Tallulah lynching, including: Will Rogers, Dr. J. Ford Hodge, Frank Raymond (eighteen-year-old itinerant artist from Iowa who spoke eloquently on behalf of the Sicilians at the inquiries, explaining the economic and voting issues that made the lynchers come after the Sicilians), Sheriff Lucas, John Wilson (lyncher–I merged him with an unnamed saloon keeper who offered free drinks to anyone who would help in the lynching), Father May (itinerant French priest from Lake Providence who spoke against the lynchers at the inquiries), Joe Evans (Francesco's employee, who spoke on behalf of the Sicilians at the inquiries), Paul and Bill Bruse (employees who also spoke on their behalf at the inquiries), Anden Severe (citizen who furnished the rope), Mr. Coleman (citizen who climbed a tree and tied the rope that hanged Cirone, Rosario, and Francesco), Mr. Blander (barber who witnessed the lynching and spoke against the lynchers at the inquiries).

In building characters, I also used American slave narratives, narratives by Tunica people recorded by Mary Haas, and diaries and fiction written by people from that part of Louisiana in that period. My attention was as much on language and culture as on history. I added a sixth Sicilian, Calogero, and allowed myself to fill in the world beyond the facts I uncovered. Indeed, in the materials I found, there was disagreement over fundamental facts, including the names of the people lynched and their ages. But everyone agrees that Dr. Hodge was shot and that he recovered completely.

The materials I consulted agree that Giuseppe Difatta (age thirty-six, Italian citizen) and Carlo Difatta (age fifty-four) were both hanged in the slaughterhouse on July 20, 1899. Francesco Difatta (age thirty), Rosario Fiducia (age thirty-seven), and a third person whose name might have been Cerami or Cirone Fiducia or Giovanni Cirano or Cerano (and whose age might have been twenty-three or thirteen, Italian citizen) were dragged from the jailhouse and hanged from a cottonwood tree outside the courthouse later the same night. All the bodies were so riddled with bullets that they were disfigured almost beyond recognition.

There were two more Italians living in Milliken's Bend, Giuseppe Defina and his son Salvatore. Buck Collins helped them escape being lynched that night by taking them in his boat to Vicksburg.

That was the sum total of Italians living in Madison Parish in 1899.

This is a work of fiction. The references aided me in so many ways, but, ultimately, the personalities and words of the characters in this story, both Italian and not, are, with only few exceptions, a product of my imagination, since I found little information on any of them.

Now, after I've read so much, and have tried to imagine what life was like then, the economic motivations for lynchings seem obvious to me. But they were not presented like that when I was in school. Indeed, racism was presented as something incomprehensible. Sometimes I think we like to imagine that evil is like a disease—it strikes at random and for no good reason. But the evil behind lynchings in the American Reconstruction period was often based on people's trying to maintain their wealth and power. That's far worse than a disease—that's a calculated decision. That's chosen evil.

This is a story that hurts. But pain isn't always bad. Pain can help us gain the empathy that compels us to act decently. We can't afford to be ignorant about bigotry. Not in our history. Not in our present day.

NOTES ON RESEARCH

There are documents in both English and Italian about the Tallulah lynching, in the form of newspaper articles (many available online) and diplomatic letters and depositions between the United States and the Italian governments from July 26, 1899, to December 4, 1900. A fine article about it, "Guns, Goats, and Italians: The Tallulah Lynching of 1899," by Edward F. Haas, appeared in *North Louisiana Historical Association* 13 (Summer 1982) and is available on this Web site: www.rootsweb.ancestry.com/~lamadiso/articles/lynchings.htm.

There are also numerous scholarly articles about lynching in general and about specific lynchings, the vast majority of them of African Americans, but some of Italians. Beyond the eleven Sicilians murdered in March of 1891 in New Orleans (about which there are many articles), three were killed in May of 1891 in Wheeling, West Virginia; four in June 1892 in Seattle, Washington; one in Denver, Colorado, in 1893; another three in Hahnville, Louisiana, in 1896. And others.

Newspaper articles called Italians "treacherous" and "bloodthirsty" with a "natural propensity toward crime." A Seattle newspaper claimed all Italians carried stilettos. A fine article to consult is "The Lynching of Sicilian Immigrants in the American South, 1886–1910," by Clive Webb, in the journal *American Nineteenth Century History* 3, no. 1 (Spring 2002): 45–76. For my Italian-speaking readers, a superb book is *Corda e sapone: storie di linciaggi degli italiani negli Stati Uniti,* by Patrizia Salvetti (Rome: Donzelli, 2003). An article that offers an economic analysis of the situations surrounding this story is "Italian Immigration in the State of Louisiana: Its Causes, Effects, and Results," by Paolo Giordano, in *Italian Americana* 5, no. 2 (1979): 160–177. And a very fine book with multiple articles about the racial status and relations of the Italians in America is *Are Italians White? How Race Is Made in America,* edited by Jennifer Guglielmo and Salvatore Salerno (New York: Routledge, 2003). You can access some particularly relevant parts of this book online at: books.google.com. Type in "Are Italians White?" in Search Books. Click on the title in Search Results. Go to page 60.

Some final remarks about language. First, please note that *Negro* was the unbiased term for an African American during the time period of this novel. For Joseph's speech and stories, I relied heavily on the work of the linguist Mary Haas. With regard to Southern speech, I found multiple inconsistencies of usage in the original works I consulted, both by African Americans and whites. And while inconsistency is not uncommon in actual speech, it doesn't always ring true in fiction (ironically). So I turned to academic works for guidance, including several articles by John Rickford and the books *African-American English: Structure, History, and Use*, edited by Solikoko Mufwene, John Rickford, Guy Bailey, and John Baugh (New York: Routledge, 1998) and *English in the Southern United States*, edited by Stephen Nagle and Sara Sanders (Cambridge: Cambridge University Press, 2003).

The spelling of speech does not reflect pronunciation. So just like *going to* would be pronounced "gonna" in many contexts, *sir* will be pronounced "suh" in many contexts. I'm counting on readers to let their eyes and ears work together as they read.

ACKNOWLEDGMENTS

Thanks to my family, Joseph Bruchac, Libby Crissey, Maurice Eldridge, Alice Galenson, Annette and Jack Hoeksema, Roberta Hofmann, Gabriel Kroch, Lisa Lee, Samara Leist, Michael Pfeifer, John Rickford, Lou Riley, and Richard Tchen. Thanks also to Iris Broudy and to my editorial team, Ruth Homberg, Caroline Meckler, and, especially, to Wendy Lamb, ever constant in her startling insights and firm support. And a final thank-you to Patricia McKissack, for her wonderful work and for lending me her name.

DONNA JO NAPOLI is the author of many distinguished books for young readers, among them *The Great God Pan, Daughter of Venice, Crazy Jack, The Magic Circle, Zel, Sirena, Breath, Bound, Stones in Water, Hush: An Irish Princess's Tale*, and, most recently for Wendy Lamb Books, *The King of Mulberry Street*. She has a BA in mathematics and a PhD in Romance linguistics from Harvard University and has taught widely at major universities in America and abroad. She has five children and one grandson and lives in Swarthmore, Pennsylvania, where she is a professor of linguistics at Swarthmore College. You can visit her on the Web at www.donnajonapoli.com.